Jon and Lale's Dance

A novel

By Connie Williams

Jon and Lale's Dance

A novel by the author of

Green Emily's Blues

AWAP
A Williams Acorn Publication

Jon and Lale's Dance is a work of fiction. Names, characters, place, and or incidents either are products of the author's imagination or used fictitiously. Any resemblance to actual events, origin of locales or persons living or dead, is entirely coincidental.

Book design by C-Mae

ISBN: 978069279998-7

Printed in the United States of America

Appreciation to: My family members both nuclear and extended for their love and patience. The manifestation of this work could not have taken form without them. And to the one important team member/partner who was my eyes and ears when I was totally out of steam:

Robbie.

This book is dedicated to my love ones exclusively.

When I first began writing Jon and Lale's Dance,

the beloved parents, Jones and Lille were both with us.

They have since departed for heaven within only four

months apart.

My dearly beloved daughter, Connie Maria and

our dearly beloved sister, Gail Marie are now in heaven

with our parents.

Jon and Lale's Dance is a heart wrenching and compelling story of genuine family devotion and hope, as the members are required to come to terms with the eventual veracity of death, while facing life storms and struggles of the twenty-first century.

Characters

Jon Cam Smalls Sr., the ailing father
Lale, the ailing mother
Topia, trying to remain strong
Emmy, a University conflict
Lionel, suffers a tragic loss
Reynolds, has to make a vital decision
Roselyn, faced with a legal battle
Rudy, demonstrates Christian determination
Ailey, her undisclosed health condition
Alice, living away
Jon Cam Jr., skillful and wry
Lewis, Jon Cam Sr.'s right hand
Karl, Jon Cam Sr.'s left hand
Jenna, the youngest

1

*I*n September 2005, at age eighty-four, as he lay in the hospital bed, Jon Cam Smalls Sr. made some joke of his condition, like there was no fall, and there's no pain, and no broken hip, and no punctured lung— no! No pain at all. But Daddy knew how he got here in Room 204 at Union Memorial Hospital. He knew they were talking about him, tight lipped and critically—even cynically, especially the younger ones. He imagined what they whispered in the group about him: He should be ashamed—with his *old self* still carrying on in such a way. He'll swear he's all right. And that he'll be back on his feet in no time.

He imagined the oldest one saying: We need to talk make some decisions while all of us are all together. The older ones can mostly make the decision about him and her. It's hard to talk to him. You know he thinks he knows everything. He won't listen to reason.

If we postpone the decision, it'll be hard to get everybody together again with everybody so busy and going their own separate ways and all. It's not the best time right now in light of what's happened and all but it's not like we can put it off either.

Now he'll be in the hospital for quite a spell. The doctor said. How long of a stay? He's so frail. But at least his color is good. But still he's already crippled and now this. You got a point there, the others agree in unison. You're right there. One says, this is a double whammy.   Before this, Lale was already often furious about the attention from all of us coming in and making over him while he sat in his chair at the kitchen table and did nothing. *Now it'll be worse*. After all she is ill herself: Beginning signs of dementia, and breast sores that Mom's decision caused the symptoms to go untreated much too long that started to continually bleed out until she absolutely could not hide them any longer. Besides, she felt if they were treated with chemotherapy, then the budget could not stand such an expense. Additionally, she completely refused to allow the doctors to "cut" on her. If they did operate on her, she said, there were no guarantees that all of the sores would be removed (she rejected the fact that the sores were malignant cells). She did not want to lose her breast; she says she wanted to keep her dignity.

And you know how she talks: It's my house, my husband, our business; we don't need you all coming in and out. Now it's going to be worse.

It sure will. She'll have a fit. She'll go off. Somebody will have to be there just about all the time-- to keep her off of him.

You know we can't let her hear you. And if you tell him anything, he'll go right back and tell her. You know how he is. So we can't say anything right now— no. Not right now. He'll act like he's still the prince at the ball. He's just too damn arrogant—too arrogant for his own damn good—poor thing. It's a shame.

The group talked of these ideas about him and he knew "fool" well that they were. After all he knew his children. He felt he knew more about their thinking than they knew themselves. He knew what they were saying: that he is old and pitiful.

After all it was he who had gotten out of bed in the middle of the night, after the music, the laughter, the cake the icing, the balloons, the flowers, the gifts. After being bedded down by his children, Jon sneaked pass Lale's bedroom to the front door and out to the porch to pull out his pack to smoke one of his Camels. He had been warned about it. Before now, he had always managed to blame it on Jenna in the past whenever he got caught.

"If it hadn't been for Jenna, I wasn't even going to smoke—I wasn't even thinking 'bout no cigarette, but she handed it to me. She told me, here Daddy let's smoke us one. It was hard to turn baby girl down."

But baby girl knew he was the turncoat having enticed her. When this happened "Baby Girl" was nowhere around, was in bed sleeping soundly beside her husband Jude, the very way he should have been in bed asleep with his wife, Lale. **But no!** He had attempted to do something he did in his younger days. In his younger days he always smoked a cigarette after a good party. Now he had no one to blame but himself.

It had been a wonderful humid Friday night eighty-second birthday for Lale and sixty-third wedding anniversary, and celebration. The party had left him feeling young. *His mind told him he was still vibrant.* He told himself, "My mind did **not** trick me."

In his mind, he was not old and **certainly** not pitiful. After all he still knew the hypotenuse formula, the largest side of the right triangle that he explained to his son-in-law Eddie, when asked, who was embarking upon the study of gastronomic; he knew the A= Pi (r2); he still knew "Three score and ten..." the meaning of x the unknown variable—a sign used to indicate x-ray or to indicate a "KISS" at the end of a letter. SWAK (sealed with a kiss) is what she wrote at the end of the letter she wrote to him when he was in the Army in the Philippines—a kiss—**her** kiss. He had not thought these thoughts in many, many years. Oh, yes! The **x** to indicate multiplication—indicate dimensions use between figures like "three by four inches" his father's measurement of furniture when he was a young boy helping with the upholstery in his father's shop over at Bent Hill. A man's lifetime—yes having lived "three score and ten"— plus thirteen—these thoughts swirled around in his head.

****

The Friday night celebration had now turned into Saturday morning. Five of the seven daughters and two of the five sons had responded to the emergency telephone call—in the early hours.

Lale had found him lying on the front porch faintly calling her name.   Then frantically with trembling fingers she called the oldest, Topia the one that lived close by. The oldest had called the others from the hospital. The voice on the receiver had said to them, "It's Daddy!" She hadn't needed to say much more except for where the men in the white clothes with the stretcher were taking him. They had all come--worried eyed and warm kisses on his sunken cheeks, with anxious questions about what happened. They gave strong hugs and encouragement for each other and for Lale when for the first time they saw that she did look scared—more afraid it seemed than any other time-like a fawn caught in headlights—not like the woman who ranted about the house before.

They recognized her dazed look of panic. They knew that she could not eat when he was away. They recognized helplessness in her face standing there beside his bed after the surgery of only three hours before. Then the group had moved down the hall to the waiting room to drink vending machine Cokes and talk together near the transparent window with the bright September sun shining through.

Jon understood it all. He heard the faint clink of quarters landing in the tray of the drink machine as the can sodas dropped down and slid on the slippery surface like one sliding on frozen ice as he lay in his hospital bed down the hall a short distance from them.

He lay in the hospital bed between the microorganism preventive clean sheets with his aluminum walker, which he used to get around resting in the corner nearby. It hadn't been that long between his previous hospital stay when he lay between the antiseptic sheets when he had the two surgeries. It hadn't been long since they had hovered over him wondering if he would make it—if he would pull through. This was after the first patella surgery and then the second patella surgery, and the abdomen problems occurred. It hadn't been long since his sons and daughters had huddled and whispered.

All of it now made him so tired. He longed so much to close his eyes and sleep—just rest his head on the pillow and let the sleep overtake his mind and body. He knew he could not get away with closing his eyes and pretending to sleep. He knew they would not allow him to do that. He knew also that they held the best of intentions though—they meant no harm; they meant well.

He knew about the good intentions of the ones that had come. They had been called from their homes and families when he was sick and frail, just like when he was ill before. And they intended on nursing him, seeing to it that he ate the right kind of food; the right kind of nourishment to keep him alive. They intended to nurse him almost like a mother nursing her baby until the cheeks become plump and rosy. It had been such a long battle, especially with him so difficult-so hardheaded—so stubborn. He wished with all his might to be different—more tolerant, more…. But he knew also that he could not change, not if his life depended on it; and wishing it did not make it so. They would just have to live with him and accept him the way he is.

They were called, but most of the load fell upon his oldest, Topia and the fifth child Rudy and sometimes Ailey, the ones who lived the closest. And she needed to talk about things. Topia needed to talk of how things really are. She needed to talk of the struggle with him and with her. She did not want to fight with them though. It was the wrong place, time and scene for disagreement--not at this time. It was her time to be heard. She was the leader. They could have their say later, if they needed to talk at all among themselves in their own small groups perhaps in their own places. She did not want them to pity her, even if they felt they should. As she spoke the pride and modesty came to the listener's minds, and Topia was surrounded with respect. Every one of them was headstrong and determined when it came to being heard, just like him and just like her. He knew the kind of children they had produced together—half him and half her. Each is the child of his parent. "Lord have mercy." He whispered to himself. They'll hear her—listen to her for now, but later they won't wait; they'll have their place on the floor. They'll demand to be heard, especially Rudy and Ailey. She won't be able to shut those two up for long. But poor Jenna, poor Baby Girl is most likely bawling right now, bawling like a baby, saying, "My poor daddy, my poor, poor daddy." Poor girl, but their intentions are good. Lying here in his bed he thought of them gathered in the waiting room, planning out his days.

The sun shone brightly through the transparent window of his hospital room, and he wished with all of his heart and his mind that he had remained in bed beside her the night of the fall. But he couldn't contain his great joy. It had been the celebration of life, marriage, children and sixty-three years together with the same woman. The **SAME** woman! He knew that he favored cynicism when it came to expressing his love for **that** woman. But his love for her had always run so deep—as deep as the ocean. It pained for him to even think of it now. Who else but her could stand to put up with his stubbornness, his often insensitive and sharp perception for all these years?

He had sipped a taste of "spirits" in a glass of ice—just the way he liked it. And when everyone was gone and in his mind the night was still young, he was feeling inspired to go out to the porch of the new home his second son had provided for them. The words overtook his heart—new home—second son—provided for us—had built from the ground up. He was a great son all grown up with his own wife and children, with the big and powerful job at the huge Cyber Security firm. Again, his heart swelled with overflowing emotions. He made a sigh. And upon hearing the sound, Lale took a closer look at Jon to see that he was all right.

She called to him, "Are you awake? Jon, are you all right?"

He heard but did not respond. And when he did not answer, she did not insist. His private thoughts were too overwhelming right now. They almost brought the tears. He fought them back.

That night he desired to just walk outside to the porch and stand and have a "drag" like in the old days, on his Camel cigarette while the world slept—mainly while Lale slept. He wanted to puff and watch the smoke disappear while gazing at the stars, the Little Dipper, the Big Dipper; the Milky Way. He imagined himself answering the nightly owl and hearing a hundred crickets sing together. He wanted to listen for the birds that may have been twittering in the trees. He would steady himself by holding onto the porch column with one hand and hold his cigarette between the arthritically curled fingers on the other hand. He wanted the joy of having done something all by himself once again that no one else would know about—only he alone—he and his Lord.

He wanted to stand to smoke and to remember when Lale was joyful in the days when all of the children were finally matured and away from the house, and he could do things all by himself. When he could walk to the porch with her—when he could take her for a long drive, even when it was just up the highway 74 to Gastonia, to the fabric store to purchase material for the upholstery shop, just the two of them in the old gray Bonneville. This was before when they still lived in the old house, the one on the other side of town in Bright Town at Fairley, the one where four of the children were birthed right there at home. Time seems to have totally gotten away from them like one letting go of a kite string and it escaping into the clouds, like the day turning into night before one can turn around. They didn't walk out to the porch to sit together, or wave to the passerby's. They didn't share porch talk or listen for the noon whistle at the Alameda mill. They didn't set the clock by the deliverance of the mail—time had left them. Now he hardly even made it out of bed, he hardly removed his pajamas and dressed before noon to sit in his chair by the kitchen table to sit, argue with her, stare—and nap.

Since the kneecap surgery, his movement lacked agility; however, his mind was still as keen as ever. So when he was awake, his stare was not an absent-minded one. Behind his stare were his deep penetrating thoughts, which wavered between the conscious daily fight at home with her condition, his own illness, his children, and the subconscious, between his survival in New Guinea and the memory of the war he fought in the

Philippines in 1943, WWII. It had always been hard—
his battles, but he had survived. And he would make up
his mind to survive this too, if not for himself—for her.
He knew they all needed him, especially Lale--She
needed him the most—cripple as he is he would will his
mind to think rationally, logically and survive!

At that moment he felt a warm slim but strong
hand cuff over his forehead. The hand seemed to draw
his thoughts from the past to the present to pull him in
like a drowning man panting to be pulled in out of deep
water. It put him in touch with the here and now. He
didn't open his eyes, not even a little bit. It was one of
his sons leaning in close to him and checking his
breathing. Yes it was a slim hand, and he could therefore
figure out which son it was. Then he heard a whisper in
his left ear.
"I love you Dad."
He was now confident of which one it was. It was
Jon Cam Jr., his child named for him. It warmed his
heart all over again, but he did not move. But then he
intended to open his eyes. Before he had a chance to
open his eyes, he realized that his son had gone over to
his mother, Lale, who was now dozing again in a chair
near Jon's bedside; Jon Cam Jr. had caressed her and
moved away from the bedside to join the huddle.

And now there were eight in the group, and it was
reckoned that although they all had been called still four
had not come. The oldest continued with her say—
asking the question, had anybody heard from Lionel,
Reynolds, Roselyn and Emmy? Turning to each other
with their repetitive expressions of genuine concern the

consensus was that the four had not taken to heart and responded—nor had the two spouses.

Four of the children lived away; and one of the four who had not come lived the farthest away, three lived in the Queen City, and Roselyn lived in another state across the North Carolina line. The two powerful ones—especially the powerful one who lived on Lake Wyle, he missed these two children the most. He knew he needed to keep these feelings completely under wraps. He knew he dared not allow the others to discover his emotional attachment with these two of his children. He said to himself: a man has a right to have an attachment especially with his **oldest** son. He mostly got a chance to see them on special occasions like anniversaries, and holidays like the Fourth of July, or Thanksgiving; sometimes not even then.

But he understood how much responsibility Roselyn must have with such a job in the corporate world—the planning, the meetings, the traveling, all the components of big business, management and sells. Seemed she was out of town more than she was in. Sometimes, just the thought of it all completely boggled his mind when he thought of it as he sat and often slept.

He had lost touch with Lionel when he served in the Marine Corp during the Vietnam War. He knew they had so much in common—fighting a war. He wished they could talk and compare experiences, the battles, the fears, the lonely days and nights—the longing for home and the good smell of bread baking in an oven. There was so much to be said that hadn't been said, but like Roselyn, Lionel was inundated with the responsibilities of the job— his UPS service supervisory administrative responsibilities, and hers CEO of sells in cost-effective media for advertisement.

None of the siblings had heard from Emmy moreover; like Lionel and Reynolds, she too now lived in the Queen City. She had married young, moved away then returned some years later. Her return home had been a productive one beginning a career in academia and then she remarried Eddie Samuels. He supposed it was foolish of him to think of his children in the manner he did when they were little children at his feet. He remembered Emmy mostly in this way; her marrying so young, she had not been a child for long at all. When his children were young, there was ever hardly any time for play, and now there is too much time for him but not for his children.

All of their responsibilities—it all made him think of his own small upholstery shop he built with his own two hands, he and his sons, Jon Cam, Lewis and Karl in the back yard—the long nightly hours of hard work, pulling and sewing that old hard material that caused his wrist to become bent and weak, and his fingers curled with rheumatoid arthritis. Now he can barely use his hands. He remembered the powerful white man who wanted to invest in a modern day state-of-the-arts upholstery shop with materials and display room-the complete mechanisms. Such things just made him uneasy.

He knew though that his sons had always helped him in the little shop – especially Jon Cam Jr. with his quiet hard-working demeanor, seemed he always knew exactly which turns to make whether it was to the right or the left when tying down those springs in chairs he upholstered; like Jon Cam, he knew Lewis was his right hand when he had a furniture deadline, and like Lewis, Karl was his left hand when he was restoring automobile seats. After returning home from the Marines, Lionel sometimes managed to pitch in; together they got the job done. But a mega owned business was totally different. He didn't know if he would be able to completely depend on his sons who were still young and still wild, still 'sowing their wild oats' at the time and likely to become frustrated and break free of the confining ropes of constant hard work. And later when Lewis went off to East Carolina and Karl went to school at Wingate he was mostly on his own in his shop. He began to think and think and think as he lay in the hospital bed while his children met in the group. It made him so tired, so he made up his mind to put it aside for now. He decided this was not the place to rehash such matters, after all, that was then and this is now.

2

*S*o Topia the oldest talked of the illnesses—

of Jon and of Lale, the convalescence, the need to band together, the responsibilities of the young siblings, the commitment of the older ones, what's going to occur on each and every day.

"Consequently, it's not like we are a bunch of carefree souls without our own houses, spouses and jobs. Rudy works for long hours in the mortgage department with customers breathing down her neck, and she has a husband;   Jenna's over yonder with her head in computers all day; Ailey works out of town and has to make that long commute every day." She continued to go down the line citing each one's obligations. "You *guys* all have wives, husbands and children, so I know how difficult it's going to be to try to come here to help out. I certainly don't have it easy on my job. You know how it is with the school system and all those hard-headed chaps that don't want to do the right thing—what the teacher tells them." She paused, "Whew!"

"It's not going to be easy and it's not going to get any better—this is just the beginning." Topia told them about these things. Meanwhile they were silent and listening and   the love was in her voice. She felt the circumstances was that they had to run things among the family members alone because she knew the frustration of relying on outsiders—there was just too much preparation in that, too many struggles of anticipation that may or may not happen. Yet the huddle had not been able to make any concrete decision about their parents, Jon and Lale.

****

No one saw it coming, when suddenly Topia's monologue was brought to a hush by a nurse who suddenly appeared and speaking hurriedly in an obviously quavering voice. She asked if this was the Smalls family. And learning that indeed it was they, she informed them of some horrifying news: Lionel Smalls and his best friend Will had been in a serious accident on Highway 74 near Round Hills, in Morristown, and they were being brought into the Union Memorial Hospital.

The shock of the news rendered the group speechless as they moved in a scurrying rush to the emergency area of the hospital when nurses in white scrambled to meet the two stretchers being brought in, and rolled down the hallway then disappeared behind closed Intensive Care Unit doors just as quickly.

Topia could not squeeze any words from her mouth. The sight of the two swallowed up any utterances; it was just too overwhelming. As usual, Rudy and Alice held onto each other's hands and stared into each other's eyes in total disbelief, and two of the sons, Lewis and Karl moved to Jon's room to gather around the parents. Jenna and Ailey stood together. Jon Cam remained at his sister's side in an attempt to comfort Topia as they all awaited silently with their minds going off in a hundred different directions; they waited helplessly for some news of the injured—for someone to tell them what had happened.

Time was moving along slowly as the clock watchers paced across the tile floor of the hospital waiting room and rung their hands in attempts to keep some sense of control in their agony. It didn't seem possible yet two and a half hours had now passed. Darkness had replaced where the daylight had been. The long hand on the clock reached its home at twelve, and the short hand settled on eight—still there was no word.

3

*L*ionel had not gone directly home after his parents' anniversary celebration the night before. He was still in the festive mood; so instead, as soon as he reached the Queen City, he made one of his regular appearances at the Excelsior night club where he continued the celebration. When he finally reached home in the early morning just as he told himself, "I've got to get some shut-eye," he hit the answering machine button hearing Topia's message and learning of his father's surgery. And only hours earlier, just before his accident, he was endeavoring to be the good son. He was in route from Mecklenburg County to Morristown to his ailing father's side. Although relationships between he and his father were strained and had been that way for some time, he knew his heart could not allow the day to pass without seeing his father, Jon.

Before his attempt to strike out on the highway heading east from the big city, he had stopped by to say hello and possibly chat with Will, his best running buddy, who had graduated high school with him and who knew more about him, he felt, than most, Lionel being a single man. And although life had taken them their separate ways after high school, still they had managed to remain good friends.

Just as he was leaving for Morristown, ironically Will had asked to ride along, give his best regards to Mr. Smalls and the family, and during the visit see his own sister who lived close by on the Hill. Lionel welcomed the company; in his mind the ride would be good for another one of their soul to soul talks. He always enjoyed their camaraderie. He felt that Will did not completely understand the change in him when he said, "War changes a man." Will couldn't know the particular irritation he felt in his heart—the memory that only a soldier knows of jumping from an aircraft with an AK Forty-Seven strapped across his back, ammunition in a backpack, landing in a field from the enemy, and treading through water for days with leaches that eventually parasite one's body. His memory was weighted with the sight of the fearless Vietnamese and the relentless attacks. Yes! War had changed him. Only a man of iron wouldn't be changed.

However, Will *did* know about Lionel's frustration with his father. He had certainly talked about it plenty. He blamed the government for his irrevocable war experiences, but he knew that Lionel blamed his father for his childhood ones—for not taking more of an interest in him, an interest that only a father could have provided when he was young and tender, and the two of them played on the baseball team.   Only a father would have been told about the time he walked home from the baseball game and was accosted by a drunk driver in a Chevrolet who abruptly stopped beside him, placed a gun to his temple demanding, "Drink this liquor boy, or I'll blow your brains out!" Afterwards he ran out of breath and frantically to home. Unfortunately, by the time he saw his father again, the next day, the fright as well as the anxiety had already been forced from his mind and body. The only thing left was indignation toward an absent father who was always working. Neither was he happy with the way he felt his mother neglected him during his youth. In fact he had never really gotten over it.

Life had not been easy for him coming up the third child of twelve. He grew up fast, went off to A&T College in Greensboro and was soon drafted into the military. His service to his country, while in the Marine Corp during the Vietnam War seemed to have gone unnoticed like his service to his family as a teenager and the oldest male sibling-the responsibilities which fell upon his shoulders for the younger children under him— his service when he played on the baseball team—the service of raising the family name instead of tearing it down, gaining respect so that people in the community might say: fine family, wonderful son-proud father when he came as a spectator to the field to see his oldest son play. Lionel felt it was widely believed that a child belongs to his father-the child while growing up is worth no more than the father's worth.   But Jon was preoccupied with other matters. He never showed up— not once. His father didn't engage in any community organizations.   Through his father's absence, Lionel suffered. Back then as he gazed around the field from the baseball diamond at other fathers who had come in support of their sons, Will's father for example. Lionel experienced great humiliation not easily erased because his father's face he so longed to see was not among the crowd. So if his childhood experiences had not already hardened his heart, military training and carrying an AK Magnum 47 certainly didn't help matters, nor improve many feelings of compassion. It served to train him at suppressing his emotions in most matters when it came to his mother and father. Indeed he loved his parents, but he did not understand either one of them. In his younger days, right after returning to the U.S. from Vietnam, at some points, their actions were so devastating to him. Realizing that at some point in life, most children are ashamed of their parents for one thing or another, but he was so ashamed of them, that he only managed to escape his pain through the night club scene and drown his sorrow in the use of a good stiff Pinch cocktail. Although he did not desire to because he adored the family scene with his siblings and his parents, he mostly isolated himself from them to save his own sense of pride and manhood.

Will knew that Lionel's parents and the military had harmed the **good** man deeply—a man who would render the shirt from his very own back for someone in need of it. Will confessed many times to him that he felt he understood the words, war changes a man. Additionally, he also knew that *life* changes a man too. He felt his friend was speaking of the war, which cut through his flesh and penetrated his soul; not the war he fought in the foreign country and returned home from, but the one going on within his own paining heart.

*** *** ** *

As time wore on Cam knew that he needed to persuade Topia to sit and rest. After all, she is not a young woman; all of us have some age on us he thought to himself.

"Why don't we sit there? You're going to wear yourself out." He said to her motioning toward a soft chair in the corner of the waiting room. In spite of his attempt to protect and care for her, he did not want to wrestle with her strong will, her might.

She just kept clutching her pocketbook close to her breast, clearing her throat and squeezing her lips tightly into a narrow line. She finally managed to utter, "Just let me stand. You can sit. I'm all right; let me stand."

Minutes later, one nurse who knew Topia, who had finished Winchester school with her appeared in the hallway and the huddle rushed to her, surrounding her. "I just left the two. I don't believe it is as bad as it looks. It's going to be all right." She finally said. It was obvious that she was choosing her words thoughtfully-carefully, and not wanting to give any false hope; she was interrupted before she had a chance to say any more.

Rudy and Alice stood there; they were both trying to talk at the same time. "Tell us about our brother; how is Lionel?" They demanded. "How's Will?"

Cam spoke with glazed fearful eyes, "They looked pretty banged up to me; it looked bad." He held on to Topia as he talked for her.

Topia still couldn't speak. She stood there tightly squeezing her purse with one hand and the other one held over her mouth, her lips pressed together tightly into a narrow line as if she was trying to keep those terrible, frightful groans and squeals she was making from escaping, the kind that some Christians make at the onset of an invigorating, head shaking, arm lifting shout. She finally whispered, "Lord have mercy! Lord have mercy!" She broke from Cam, stopped clutching her purse when it fell to the floor. She raised her hands up to the ceiling "What in the world happened? Can somebody tell us what's going on?" These fretting and exasperating words were so hard for her to ask that they made her body move as it did when she herself was in church and overtaken with trembling of the Holy Ghost. The three left the huddle to rush to her side, pulled her close to them to console her because they saw and could not stand how it was tearing her down.

Jenna began to bawl. Fat tears ran down both of her round cheeks, and Ailey hugged her without a word. She hesitated before reciprocating the embrace then managed to pull herself away from the hold, "I've got to get out of here—get some air. I need to smoke!" Jenna said and walked hurriedly out of the waiting room like someone wading blindly through a fog.

The nurse was about to tell them the story she heard about the accident when two Morristown "black and whites" appeared. One carried some papers in his hand and they walked to the center of the waiting room.

Will's sister was with them. She looked totally bewildered. She still wore sponge rollers in her hair that stuck out from underneath a head scarf. She ran over to Topia. "Will just died, Oh Lord, Oh God! He just died!" Her chilling cry was uttered painfully and she sobbed loudly as she held her arms up to reach for Topia and put her head on Topia's shoulder. The two stood there arms wrapped around each other tightly, and with Jon Cam standing near.

"They couldn't save him-they couldn't save my brother." Her body shook like a cold shiver came over her. "I've got to go home and plan a funeral for him." She said in despair. As she pulled herself away from them and ran out of the waiting room door, Topia and the group were left standing there vulnerably.

One police officer began to speak, "We responded to the call of the accident. Your brother, Lionel's car was hit by a tractor trailer trying to make a left turn. The driver of the truck couldn't stop when the light changed. It hit the automobile on the passenger side."

By now the clock on the waiting room wall said nine fifteen. Down the hall the double doors swung open, and the doctor found his way to the family standing there waiting. He stood towering in front of them and peering down through his thick horn-rimmed glasses. He stood there with the worried eyes looking up at him with their anticipated hopes. He spoke gingerly and in a compassionate tone. He started to explain, "Your brother lost a lot of blood. His spleen was punctured, and we have operated—and able to save it. His pressure was 200 over 95, we're stabilizing it so the surgery was successful, but Lionel is in serious condition; the lost of blood required a blood transfusion. He has some internal injuries. He'll be on guarded around the clock observation."

Immediately following the doctor's news, everyone rushed to Lionel's side in the Intensive Care Unit. Leann, his girlfriend stood there at his bedside.

While the family and Leann quietly stood there viewing him sleeping heavily under sedation, Emmy made her composed entrance to be with the family to touch and hug them; provide her support and prayers and to learn about her brother's condition for herself. Afterwards she finally made her way to her father Jon Cam Sr.'s side.

4

***J*on Cam Sr.'s start in life** wasn't necessarily a meager one, but it was nevertheless difficult. Unlike other families with three-four-five-even six children, there were fifteen children in his family. The story had been told in Morris County, of how his father may have possibly had one-half of an ounce of black blood in his veins, but by all standards in the black community, anyone with white skin, blond hair and blue eyes was considered white. He was a Methodist minister owning his nine room two story home and upholstery business on Bent Hill, a mule and wagon for furniture deliveries, pigs for slaughter; including flourishing, shady fruit trees, grapevines and a bountiful garden with vegetables, all nestled on twenty acres that triangle at Skyway Drive-601, Highway 74, and Concord Highway.

His mother was a mixture of the Lumbee Tribe of North Carolina and African American.

As number five of his father's children, and many years ago when Jon was a young boy he was brought up in his father's Methodist church. Regular attendance on Sunday followed by fried chicken dinner and green apple pie was a ritual. When his parents died both well into their eighties, he did receive a family inheritance; although by then the house and property was in great ruins, still his father allotted in his will a plot of land to each of his fifteen children to build a home upon for their own individual spouses and children.

An apprentice working alongside his father as a young boy and on into his teens, Jon became naturally skilled in upholstery. Beyond that he was bright and handsome in his youth and later brought honor upon himself and family through his studies. It was said that in school his high school teachers took pride in boasting about his ingenious mind— he could master it all: algebra, science, English, French, social studies and the like. Yet he was not arrogant. In fact he grew up to be a quiet, gentle and patient man, somewhat naïve to the realities of life brought up under his father's strict Methodist religious rules for his children. Jon had a promising future: clearly marked for the great life— matriculating through education. He met and fell in love with the beautiful but domineering Lale while he was in the twelfth grade and they married soon after graduation before Jon went off to college. While a freshman at Shaw University Jon's schooling was cut short in the first year, when he fathered his and Lale's first child,

Topia.   Uncle Sam soon drafted him, and he was deployed overseas to the Philippines to fight in WWII before the second child, Emmy was born. When he returned to the states in 1945 following the war's end by age thirty-six, in 1960 he had fathered thirteen children, eight daughters (seven living) and five sons, so his opportunity to complete his post high school education unfortunately never happened.

In those days, putting food on the table for his family meant working three jobs. He drove his green and beige 1955 Buick up the Old Charlotte Highway in the morning to work from eight until four, then he drove it again to work from six to nine or ten, and back home again to work from eleven until one-two in the morning in his own twelve by twenty-four upholstery shop built in his backyard. The cycle would begin all over again the next day. This went on all week until the weekend. On weekends he was a trade instructor of upholstery for Central Piedmont Community College.

Sometimes he just needed to escape from it all, so he occasionally stopped to drink cold Budweiser and Johnny Walker with his brothers who lived on the "Hill"-- their homes he passed during the week, going to and from work built on their father's property.

No matter how hard or how long he labored, there was never enough money for anything—never enough energy for anything else except work—never enough time to do anything. When he finally fell into bed the early hours of the morning after leaving his shop, he was exhausted. So his occasional stop on the Hill was a tattered, disadvantaged and dehydrated man's stagger to a waterhole on a desert.

He knew his not coming straight home from work meant trouble between him and Lale each Friday that he stopped on Bent Hill. She just had no way of understanding his physical and mental exhaustion. She had no concept of his need—his great desire to use his intelligence.   The longing in his heart to live his dream—to build the big house for which he carefully and meticulously drew blueprints—the planned layout for use of the property left to him as his inheritance in his father's will--He felt that life had robbed him of his opportunity to matriculate—to use his 'bright' mind—complete his desire for a college degree. Now he felt life *only* afforded him the opportunity to earn his pay by the constant sweat of his brow. This he did out of love for his children and his wife. Whenever he made a nervous attempt to talk to his sweet Lale, to explain to her how he felt, the longings of the deepest part of his heart, his needs—desires, ambitions—his yearning for her compassion to listen to his voice, to share his dreams concerning his intellectual aspirations, she was always incensed in these matters.

"Don't *'nobody'* want to hear that doggone 'crap.'" This was the expression to Jon of her true love. "I'm the one who's been stuck here with all these chaps all day."

Each time her words rang in his ears, he flashed a disconsolate look in her direction; he was so tempted to allow his cynical self to take over, to criticize her usage of the double negative: **'don't nobody,'** in her sentence, but he dared not pass judgment on her now the way he would have done in his younger days—now it was his very nature to turn a death ear to the usage of her slang. Ironically what he recognized that she herself did not understand was her way of suppressing fear of the inevitable that was obvious in spite of her attempt to control it; as she was known for threatening to 'kick his gluteus' right from when they first met and married, especially when the man expressed himself with a superior vernacular.

Jon recognized that Lale ruled their children with an iron hand and ruled her husband with a lot of "lip", which if provoked could easily turn into violence against him. And when it came to the very idea of living among his people 'over yonder' on the Hill' as *she* put it—it was out of the question. She flatly refused— *flatly*. Usually Jon was too tired to hash it around and around and around again. He learned at an early age to let sleeping dog lie. His stop on the Hill spending time with his brothers was an attempt to avoid sinking into total despair.

So usually, when anything happened in the family, involving the children, Jon received it second hand, because he was away working— earning a living, meeting the upholstery deadlines, keeping a roof over their heads, putting food on the table, paying the light bill, buying kerosene to keep the house warm, and buying toys for Christmas, still owing for the ones purchased the year before when the next Christmas rolled around.

Hands: a poem for Daddy

HANDS won't end up like his
Hands old labored and smart
FINGERS curled
A piece of art.

HANDS fixed the furniture
Hands held twelve babies
FINGERS caressed Mom
Fragile skillful and delicate

HANDS hold a walking cane
Hands once held a gun
FINGERS pulled the trigger
In WWI

HANDS hold a crutch
Hands once yellow and strong
FINGERS need to be cared for
Fingernails have grown too long.

Note: Daddy actually was a WWII Veteran, but I needed
a rhyming word for "gun," so the persona here in the
HANDS poem appears in WWI.

****

As midday arrived, the casket rolled down the aisle. The elders of the church raised a song in unison: **Shall We Gather at the River,** that beautiful, beautiful river? The voices were heard throughout Blacks Memorial Presbyterian Church. Its sound rang down the aisle and out into the air of the surrounding neighborhood, as Will's family members, Lionel's family members, friends, the congregation and funeral goers filed by Will's casket taking their last view of the one whose life, it was said, had been cut short in its prime.

While the funeral took place, now out of ICU, Lionel lay in his hospital bed next to a window ironically, as destiny would have it, in the same room beside his father Jon. Leann had not come this morning because of her work schedule. She had informed him of her intentions to see him later in the afternoon. He stared out of the window and sobbed quietly with his mind on the last time he saw Will alive. He thought of how Sandy Kate his sister who died in her sleep at twenty-five days old, how she had saved him all of his life. And once again she had done so. Although he was not able to verbalize his true gratitude for fate's favor—for sparing his life and for his father's presence, he knew it would be worse if he were alone. This way, at least if he desired he could turn over and engage in some discourse with someone—even if it was a man who he felt he could not reason with. After all, he thought, when was the last time we've had any decent conversation about anything?

Being here with his father the memories surfaced of the early morning when it was necessary to drive Jon to Duke Veteran's Hospital in Raleigh after his second patella surgery when he had the stomach problems. Lionel recalled the pressure he felt in his heart when Jon kept instructing him on how to drive the vehicle—"I believe you missed a turn didn't you?   You where supposed to turn back yonder." Where and even how to stop—"Look out for that stop sign, you're going too fast to stop aren't you?" "Look out for the police; they patrol these parts regularly up here in Durham you know."   He asked himself, was I doing anything wrong—No! It had been an excruciating event both to Raleigh and back home for Lionel, and difficult for him to hold his tongue. Holding his tongue he realized removed that Constitutional right any war veteran such as himself should be privy of even in a discourse with his father. After all as a paratrooper having 'fought' in a war and therefore having lived a little himself, he knew something as simple as the inner state highway like the back of his hand. Besides he was Lale's son and without a doubt had her quick trash-talking tongue, therefore 'biting' it was to say the least—difficult. But he did not wish to injure an ailing old man. It was as if Jon felt his son did not have any social or navigation skills or sense of direction at all—any "know-how."   Lionel felt his father was the kind of man who felt he knew *everything* about *everything*. Yet still, in his heart, now, Lionel felt he needed the comfort of someone's words—even if it had to be Jon Cam Sr.'s words.

Jon's concerns were mixed: He wondered about his son Reynolds' absence; why had he not come to see him—he still had not been told about Will's passing. Every precaution had been taken to guard Jon's heart, weak as he was no one wanted to cause a heart attack: when the flow of oxygen-rich blood to a section of heart muscle suddenly becomes blocked and the heart can't get oxygen. His knowledge of Lionel's condition was quite enough for him to worry about. Now he wondered about Lionel's state of mind. So finally he spoke with the only words he felt might have some meaning, right now.

"Do you have pain?' and at first he did not think his son heard his words. He repeated them, "Are you in any pain?" He knew he had to be careful not to cause his son mental anguish, but he also knew he didn't need to cause his own heart to increase its palpitation. So after a moment the silence fell away when Lionel turned to face his father—to break the wall between them to respond to his question. He turned over to acknowledge that he had heard, to look at him, and their talk began.

Jon said, "I believe it was about this time of the year when I left the states, headed for that Army base in California before they sent me to Australia in 1942. I was supposed to go to Tennessee but I came back to North Carolina with Lale, she was carrying Emmy and didn't feel well; it caused me to go AWAL. Good Enough Island, South Pacific, then to New Ghenea, groomed at the 33rd Division invaded the Philippines then in 1945 the war was over. They talked from mid day to sun down.

****

Lionel wanted with all of his might to mask the pain and psychological focus from his good friend Will. It was so difficult not to talk about him, to Jon, but as soon as his life was no longer in danger and he was out of ICU, the family had assured his silence for his father's guarded condition. He asked himself 'How could this have happened to such a good, good fellow.' He chose in his mind to refer to Will as a fellow, he was like a baby brother to me—Oh God!' Now I'm left with no one. He thought. In his mind's eye he could envision all of the long talks and long drives, the university parties, high school days the two of them had shared together; those were the good times.

Now he has to go on without his good friend. He thought of his girlfriend, the good woman, who had continued to be by his side through his entire hospital ordeal. At that moment he thought, the fact of the matter is, 'the girl' (and he now thought of her, as the young girl she was when they first met), she has stood beside me for a lifetime—during my college stay—during my military stay—even when I tested the waters of other relationships—she waited. "I need to marry Leann he confessed to himself; yes, I need to marry that woman." His heart felt good—his mind needed the change of ideas. He almost said them out loud just to have them feel good on his tongue in saying them.

5

*W*hile the family members struggled with
the painful occurrences, the events were unparalleled
with the one who had finally gone to her father's and her
brother's side. Being there with the family did provide a
sense of peace for Emmy during her ordeal. Although
she knew she could not discuss it with her father; and
she did not wish to open up to *all* of her siblings—she
felt some perhaps would not provide the compassion she
felt she favored. She knew how she was viewed:
Practically a family deserter. The family does not
quickly forgive those considered its traitors, who jumped
the departing train without looking back, consequently
leaving behind the primary unit. But the long awaited
return in her eyes had promised some strange fantasy to

change the motivation of her kin by her own set example of experiences, or at least for the small few siblings who might half way be on her side. Yet being in their presence somehow helped her. So she took the strictest measures to avoid having to talk to any family members about her latest University experience until she absolutely had to. Although she was completely saddened by the loss of Will and the delicacy of Lionel's condition for which she sent up many silent prayers, nevertheless, she had been absolutely subdued by the riveted events already occupying their minds. But she entirely knew her secret had already become blatantly known through the grapevine—the family members were being careful and kind not to mention it when she had been around, but there was a look of "knowing" in the eyes that veered at her when her peripheral vision was heightened and accurate.

Any news that was learned about the family members, it usually spread, by word of mouth, like wildfire. The locals said: *Emmy was notified in an email that the University would not be inviting her back to the part-time professorship and the writing course curriculum because of a "more advanced pool of candidates for the academic year who better understood the multimodal curriculum."*

Although Emmy had made a prior decision to not return in the fall semester because of three rationales: Her age, her health, and her desire to become completely retired so as to now use her time to write— complete those manuscripts she had to postpone while she was lecturing. Her intension was to notify the University over the summer months before the fall semester. But now she had been notified, she felt, in this uncaring and disrespectful manner even in light of the dedication and hard work of the last twelve years at the University of her Alma Mater, where she graduated receiving the Master's Degree in Education. She was incensed, and she immediately without having to give it much before thought, as she followed the philosophy of two-mindedness (of should I or shouldn't I)—but there was not an ounce of indecisiveness, so she *directed* a lengthy, contemptuously charged and mocking email to the administration.

Her subject line read: **What I'm happy to share about myself, hopefully will serve to (allegedly)** *"help strengthen"* **the department—my resignation!**

It further read: This notification is for the following reasons: In an email to me the Department allegedly claims: You do not have a clear understanding of the department multimodal, academic, genre oriented/curriculum.

I find this illogical and bogus because it is evident that **I** understood the multimodal, academic, genre-oriented curriculum well for the recent Southern Accreditation of Colleges and Schools (SACS) assessments; I received written kudos from the department for my students' E-portfolio; URLs and was offered, (I add ironically) a course to teach in the spring. In fact, Dan Enenen asked my permission to use my students' multimodal project in the Faculty Training Center. This makes no sense even to the average intelligence; if in fact I did not understand the curriculum, then why would the Writing and Rhetoric Department offer a contract to teach for which I accepted and signed? Yet suddenly, I do not understand the curriculum. Then why was my Syllabus approved?

The department also alleged: Your student comments were not good; your evaluations were the lowest for the department. This too is illogical and **totally false**—my scores' mean was 3.04-3.75 out of a 4.0 for fall. In an English Department faculty meeting, it was once said by a top administrator, ones (1s are low and would be a problem if it persisted)? Specifically, both my fall discourse community of classes had some *special life and learning needs*, for which I discussed and requested assistance from the department administration and the Dean to help resolve those issues and although there were difficult students to teach with these special needs, my evaluations were in the 3.50 range out of a 4.0.

The department further alleged: While your teaching methods would serve other institutions' writing programs, they no longer serve our multimodal, academic, genre-oriented curriculum.

Again, I say considering ethos, pathos, and logos, your claim is not credible, certainly not logical and does not show a compassion for persuasion. With all of these allegations, for example according to you: my unclear understanding of the department curriculum, poor teaching practices and dismal student relationships, ironically, not once has there been during the semester a students' complaint voiced to the department; neither do students reveal negativity in their Midterm Reflections nor the Final Reflections.

If in fact all of these allegedly negative variables existed, I truly KNOW I would have been "summoned" by the Department heads to Administration "and immediately FIRED on the

spot!" The mediocrity you speak of would not have been tolerated, you know this as well as I, that it would not have taken you "twelve years" to make a discovery if I do not have a clear understanding of the curriculum.

If in fact the University did not wish to offer a contract after my twelve-year career, it is believed, if we consider pathos, there should have been a more respectful and gracious method of communication as opposed to the disrespectful and condescending (drummed up) method of allegations such as, I did not understand the curriculum. I beg to wonder, is this your communicative method to all those you wish to transition out of the department, or is this the method used when you wish to transition certain groups out of the department?

As a retired veteran from another educational system, I am fortunate to have a steady income, but for those less fortunate, who did the work, were depending upon a continued position, I can't help but wonder about them.

Let's again apply ethos and logos. In that period of time—twelve years, there have been three Ph. D's in administration who have offered contracts to me to continue a teaching position for which I accepted and signed a contract.

I am aware that there may have been **twice** in **a twelve-year teaching career** here at the University that it was necessary for me to speak with administration at a student's request/concern that were resolved amicably- **-those odds are about as good as they get.**

I am aware that my instructor/student relationship is not a unique situation and that struggles do arise; however, mine are not to a greater degree than any other instructors'. In fact they are at a lesser degree when compared to some of the other instructors. Instructors do share their personal employment-related stories with each other that I do know about; and I do know that there have been times that you (the Department) have had to have legal counsel for some of these cases involving other instructors that supposedly "know your curriculum supposedly as you say better than I do."

The   department   says: There is a competitive pool of applicants as one rationale for not offering a contract to me   in   the   fall.

In a meeting following your email, I *did not* request to be called back to teach here in the fall semester. However, my reasons for the meeting seemed to have been **consistently and deliberately misinterpreted by the Department** as if you were endeavoring to make it appear that I was begging to be called back. **How Ridiculous!** That was the most humiliating and the most ludicrous scene I'd ever been involved in, in my professional career, much to say, in my life, even before becoming a professional.

While teaching at the University I am a thirty plus years retired veteran instructor from a distinguished North Carolina School system—I retired from the before mentioned school system *with honors*, mind you.

In my email to the department, *I **did** request the negative comments about my teaching practices be removed, and perhaps a different communication should be issued listing my recently excellent teaching evaluation* because the allegations about other candidates knowing the curriculum better than I are false, serve to hurt and discredit the caliber of "hard" professional and prestigious work I **know** I have performed here at the University of my Alma Mater where I received my Master's in Education degree. Additionally I am a Writing Fellow here at the University.

I find it remarkable that you, the Writing and Rhetoric Program, are willing to capitulate through the remaining of this academic semester, February, March, April and May, in light of such alleged standards that you claim. This, too, to me would seem illogical and ludicrous. If my performance is below expectations, what would seem, a solution is to bring in from your 'better pool of applicants', one who best understands your curriculum, and allow that one to take over my position and finish out the months of February, March, April and May—this spring semester.

In good conscience I will not allow myself to reflect such an "allegedly" unfavorable credit (as you claim) upon the FYW program, or myself. Therefore, I resign my position as of today, February 6. In a layman's terms: **I QUIT!**

With all due respect,
I remain, Emmy Samuels.

Then she hit the **SEND** command on her computer sending the email to LISTSERV.
Refer to: *Appendix I*

After sending the email, Emmy celebrated her decision by pouring herself a cup of hot peppermint tea with a splash of Bulleit Frontier Bourbon. She didn't indulge often but on an occasion such as this, it was entirely expected. She sipped it down to sooth her uneasy inflammatory arthritic knee, which she knew was partly caused by those frigid, across campus walks to lecture classes during the early morning schedules at the University.   As she sipped from her cup, it felt enormously good in her mind after all, knowing now she could officially consider herself retired. She swallowed the last sip from her cup of tea; elevated her legs onto the leather ottoman sitting in front of her soft, wide chair; picked up the cell and telephoned Reynolds to tell him all of the infinite details.

When his cell rang three times, he answered, "Hello!" And listening to Emmy talk of her experience, he questioned. "Are you going to be all right with this?"

She responded without hesitation, "Yes, as long as those ***contemptible breeds*** clear my name, you know, those remarks they included: A more competitive pool of applicants who better know the curriculum etc. Each time I think of it, it makes my blood boil. I plan to call the PhD who hired me, Dr. Nance, and my friend Dr. Vaunt suggested that I call the Dean and request to see my files."

****

Emmy was immensely thrilled when her older sister asked her about the University incident. She had no uneasiness in opening up to discuss the predicament with Topia, because she like Lale, usually instinctively alluded to a clever common sense approach in most situations. Although she didn't know exactly what her older sister would say, but chances were that she would replicate some idea of "someone done someone wrong," scenario, which was exactly how she responded.

"And when you do someone wrong it comes right back to you. So let it go. You were leaving anyway—you just wanted it to be on your own terms. Insist that they respect you! Knowing your smarts, you're too prestigious and hard working to allow them to discredit your contribution to *that* school, and how dare them communicate with you in such a snooty manner." This was her take on the situation.

Emmy thought, if discussed with Jon, he would have said *"Fight* with virtuosity!" She was certain he would have meant with her ingenuity—she was fully aware of one of his favorite sayings: *"The pen is mightier than the sword*!"

She imagined Lale would have reacted, in her usually direct and no-none-sense manner, with a lift of the head, pausing to focus her thoughts and attention; with a smack of the lips as if the words would taste good rolling off her tongue, would have exclaimed, *"You tell them where they can go with that!"*

****

6

*M*ost of the family members were too busy with the unfortunate matters of Jon's surgery, Lionel's condition, and Wills funeral; most of the others were too busy dealing with Lale's state of mind while her husband was away.

In the meanwhile, Roselyn still had not gone to her father's side. She lived a state away from her immediate family and orders at her house were given that no one was to answer the telephone unless it was a call to her new business, Make it Work Technical Service. Those who knew by reading about it in the paper or on the Net or by becoming initiated into the news, kept up the facade—in her protection to keep others from finding out.

Roselyn, a mature female of fifty-four, had risen from her deprived background to become prosperous in a world mostly unknown to the majority of her siblings. She saw the world in terms of her professional position in life as corporation CEO in Media Sells in her thirty-year working career. Before her job with the corporation, she became a top-notch sales rep for ABC, traveling weekly up and down the road but gave it all up for her family when her children whined—as children will about losing friends when they having discovered their mother was about to be transferred to Iowa, and they would have to move away from their friends. Having to change jobs and work her way up from menial jobs once again; the climb had not been an easy one—as she told herself on many occasions it is hard for a black woman with nothing, not even well intended, benevolent advice, to go from a problem to a problem solver—and now this.

As the family tragedies took place, Roselyn sat swallowed up in the soft velour couch, tensely subdued inside her living room of her waterfront estate gazing through the sliding patio doors out upon the backyard, which led to the golf course near the isthmus at Lake Wylie longing to talk to her father, to have his astute advice. Whether she took it or not was another matter. But now her endeavor was to plan her sincere account of the unfolding devastating events alone. Her thoughts took her to an earlier time which led to her unfortunate but sensitive matter. But the painful thoughts of her childhood kept penetrating into the present—when she was a girl of eight at home with her mother and father.

She thought of her hunger, her neglect; her fears during the family Saturday night fights, which sporadically led to the calling of the authorities in the wee hours of the morning after a night of her parents' consumption and disagreement. She remembered how terrified she had been on one occasion when Lale held her hands at her father, Jon's throat, promising to kill him for not coming home after work, Jon having stayed out all night on Bent Hill with his brothers.

At one point when she was a student at Smith University, it had gotten so bad at home for her, making it impossible for her to study—to concentrate; she made the decision to leave home to move and stay with Topia, the oldest. She experienced deep regret for leaving behind the siblings younger than herself. But she needed to escape for her own peace—her own sanity. Although she adored her college experience, as a math and science-major, it was difficult—almost, impossible, for her to perform at her best with all the hurtful conflict at home—all of the embarrassment—it was impossible to hide the shame—the smell of sour fried cabbage in her clothes; the cold unbearable rooms in the winters; the agonizing hot summers when the house felt like an inferno.

She too like her brother Lionel loved her parents; she honored them the way the Bible taught her: Ephesian 6:2, **Honor thy father and thy mother**, constantly rang in her memory, but there was great humiliation, the kind that tore her heart apart. She was almost glad when Uncle Sam accepted her out of Smith and into the Army before she completed college and sent to serve in Vietnam in a support assignment. Although not asked for, it was a form of escape.

Her thoughts leave the past as she wondered if the family might be discussing her. If she showed herself, they might just stand around eyeing her—in her lost weight—sizing her up—in a, she looks so sad and

what is she going to do manner. As she sat, she heard the
garage door open and her husband and daughters come
into the house. Before she had a chance to assemble
herself, to pull her tired limbs up to prepare for a
greeting, her youngest daughter accosted her.

"Tell me it's not true Mom! Tell me this is not
true!" She squeezed a newspaper in her hand and stood
in the middle of the living room floor with a look of
anger and a tone of animosity. She continued, "How
could you do such a thing to us? This is terrible, just
terrible! How could you just leave your job and agree to
relocate without as much as a discussion with us?" The
oldest daughter just stood and veered away to disguise
her look of disappointment.

Roselyn had been wondering about her siblings
and hometown folk, and coworkers. She already, on
Sunday at the church financial committee meeting, had
to address *them*. She remembered having to tell them
about the down-size at her corporation and the layoffs
because of mysteriously missing funds. The members
asked, "Should we trust her with our money? Should we
be concerned about the collection?" She told them,
"Let's get rid of the elephant in the room. I'm the same
person I was before this story broke. This thing
happened swiftly." However, she had not completely
anticipated the painful negative reaction of her own
immediate family—her *own* children. She thought, "Am
I completely sure I can make them understand what I
have had to endure out there in the white world as a
target up against two sets of laws—one for **them** and one
for us."

She turned to them now and began, "Even as a
young woman, I made an all out attempt to emulate what
I felt my parents expected of me, especially my father—

work hard, raise the family honor and morality. When I was a student at Smith College and later joined the Army and sent to serve in the Vietnam War all with an attempt to make something of my life as decently and proudly as I could. I married young to a wonderful man who I felt would stand with me in a way no one else could." She thought briefly, although his station in life had been one of middle privilege, he never seemed to hold any condescending animosity toward me for it. *He always had my back.*

She came back to the present. She continued. "It seems that everyone has a personal interest in the situation, especially my family. I do not believe anyone thinks more highly than I do about honor and integrity, as well as respect for our laws. I must admit that I have been somewhat blinded by the vision of hope—thinking that if I worked hard enough and long enough to prove myself worthy, then I can hope for betterment. I believe with all of my heart that the more a person educates the mind the more she is determined to change her environment. I have worked to that end—you well know I came from an extremely deprived background— sometimes going off to school unwashed and many times malnourished, unlike other more advantaged children who were well provided for. However, I never allow those hard-time experiences to get in the way of life challenges, life hopes and dreams to provide a better way for my family especially my children. In the words of Patrick Henry "We are apt to shut our eyes against a painful truth..." I realize perhaps at some particular point I dared to close my eyes for a moment to think that if I reached a certain plateau then destiny might be gracious enough to set in my path everything done to work in my favor as opposed to humiliation." She paused to take a deep breath.

"As a young girl coming up, I often wondered what my intelligence was destined to be used for. I never realized that envy and hate can be so strong an emotion in human beings. I used the intelligence granted to me by God Almighty to pull myself up out of nothing "per say" with the eyes of the world critically upon me. As I worked to pull myself up, I unfortunately become scorned and ridiculed as a person wanting too much for her own good." She shook her head before continuing. "Nevertheless, all I endeavored to do was to become the person I felt God wanted—using the skills and knowledge granted to me for betterment. Furthermore, in return, when asked—I felt that to whom much is given much is expected—therefore, I did not turn down those in need of my assistance."

She continued. "The man I married at a young age, that man there," and she pointed to Dwayne, " has been in every way an exemplary husband and father to both of you—giving me love and respect, unlike the mother and father I was raised by who did not always show that humility which a husband and wife reveals to each other. As a young girl growing up in our house, I can recall negative scenes of harm and spite directed toward my father from his wife—my mother. I would never treat your father in such a way. I never wanted my children to grow up under such discord. So in a thirty-four year marriage we, together, have tried to live God's plan for husband and wife for our family."

She walked over to pause and look outside, it seemed to gather her thoughts, then turned to them again. "But it would be unwise for me to overlook the urgency of the moment—what I am asking of my children and of my husband, my entire family and loyal friends. What I am asking is for your respect and understanding. I am asking for your loyalty to know that I have not committed anything knowingly wrong against the law. I had nothing to do with the missing funds. I am not a perfect person. Yet I am human, and like all humans, I have a propensity and proclivity toward indulgence. But I swear to you that my hands are clean. But because I was the female over the department, I am going to be released before some of the others who may have been directly involved in the ordeal. Of course there will be an investigation. But I have ***nothing*** to hide. I admit that I did make an unwise business approval for some of my business associates who are employed under me before scrutinizing all the documents for which I must endure the ordeals of consequences—to what extent, God only knows, and therefore, this puts my family in a precarious predicament."

Her daughters listened with great silence and interest. Her youngest daughter who had been listening more intensely jumps to her feet to interrupt, "So what are you saying Mom? Are you saying that you might be—be incarcerated—put behind bars!?" There was anxiety in her mannerism and bitterness in her protest.

"Wait Harriet…" And Roselyn's words trail off when Dwayne's, Harriet's father insist upon allowing their daughter the opportunity to vent her position. He raises his hands into the air, "Please, Please, Roselyn, let the girl speak."

"I simply want to know exactly what is going on here. Now you want us to forgive and continue to honor you—like nothing has happen now that this thing is in all of the papers. What were you thinking—I mean how can you have been so naïve?" She vigorously plops her body down onto the plush sofa causing it to make a sound.

"But, Darling, you must try to understand what I'm saying." Roselyn tries to persuade her.

"Well, that's just it *MOM*, I do understand better than you think I do."

With a tremor in her voice, Roselyn pleads, "But I want you to trust that I love you and will do everything in my Godly power to protect you as I always have. I will not allow my family to get mixed up into the middle of this thing; I promise you this. For me, there has not been any rest nor peace of mind since this happened. Darling daughter, we are all going to fall at some point in life. But my fall is not final. This fall won't be in such a way that I will be ruined or destroyed. I am trusting in my Lord to bring us through."

Roselyn's words did much to sooth the heart of her outspoken daughter. The one who had always challenged her mother—kept her, "so of speak" on her toes. The one so much like herself, but who was also like her father who questioned everything—always having to see both sides of the issue. So for now she felt she had given Harriet a little something to turn over in her mind's eye for at least a while before coming back at her again.

But, the one who sat silently on the couch—the one who was the first born—the one who remained the baby for eight years before the other still said nothing. But, hers were not a look of disapproval. Her silence spoke louder than literal utterances. There was an unmistaken proud yet tender demeanor about her, as a very young child, whose legs have become weak, reaching upward toward a love one about to pick her up.

She sat staring in her mother's direction—head to one side. She placed a hand on her forehead like she was using it to squeeze a comment out, "Okay Mom, I see where you're coming from. Okay." Shrugging her shoulders, she says softly, "All right."

Roselyn went to them, embraced them, and the four all gathered and sat down at the kitchen table to have the meal she had prepared and placed before them—tender collard greens, baked chicken, potato salad and ice tea. Dwayne stretched out his arms at the dinner table and the family locked fingers to hear the blessing of the food before taking of their meal.

****

7

*W*ill's **funeral now over** for two weeks, Jon and Lionel were both released from the hospital. Alice and her husband Allen carried out their plans to relocate to Florida where Allen took over the position as CEO of his company Allen Tech.

The family's focuses were varied: one on the care of Jon and Lale; and Lionel's announcement of his decision to marry Leann. He had said it would not be a large wedding. He and Leann's plans were to keep it simple but quaint, and all the family members were invited to attend the exchanging of vows at the Magistrate's office downtown in the Queen City, and there would be a small reception in the yard at the house on their property at Brush View Lane.

Their other centers of attention were as complex as the first ones— the avoidance of having to comment on the family secrets. On occasions on Saturday, small groups began to gather at Topia's house behind closed doors to decide on a course of action— should they or shouldn't they? Should they get involved? Or shouldn't they get involved?

Topia spoke, "To strangers that wouldn't have any vested interest in the situation, the answer might seem elementary. But for us who unfortunately have to live in this town to have to make a decision seriously, this is tremendously hard." The others, Rudy the savings and loan supervisor, Ailey the corrections officer, Jenna the research analysis, and Cam a supervisor in production of chemical products knew that the oldest was about to talk for some time. Therefore, Rudy, Ailey and Jenna settled on chairs, legs were crossed or curled up, Cam mixed a drink, and he and Jenna lit a cigarette all-readying for her monologue. Topia a teacher's assistant at the local Bent Hill Elementary Schools was a pack rat—hoarded everything that anyone had ever given her hardly ever throwing any of the "vintage items" teachers' hand-me-downs throw away given to her at the end of the school year. Objects not given to her, she collected at the Walmart Supercenter blue-light specials: stuffed dolls, stuffed animals, books, ceramics such as stoneware, china, pottery—stuff.

She moved to the kitchen to situate her throne, a high-back stool at the kitchen counter where she could be seen and heard from all angles—the living room which opened into the kitchen. Sitting down she balanced her feet onto the rim of the stool, then pushed aside some of the ceramic objects—angels with wings, boys and girls wearing red and white choir robes, plastic bottles of paint—brushes that she had been tinkering with earlier. She placed these objects into a box and set them aside near a glass tray, which held dusty plastic fruit. Resting her elbows onto the counter she folded her two hands as if she was about to pray; then rested her head against her hands.

"Listen to this y'all." Topia said with a tone of cynicism and everyone's attention upon her. "This ain't no laughing matter— this s--- is serious. You know we have always believed in and always been able to take care of our own—even when they do something stupid. Like that time Lionel got into a fight with that 'Jive Turkey' on his job, and we had to go over there and bring his a-- home or he was about to do some serious damage to that poor guy for calling him out of his name. Cam I know you remember how you have acted the fool too, and I've had to go and rescue you."

Jon Cam nodded his head in agreement, grinned from the side of his mouth, revealing some of his teeth, and then took a sip from his glass, puffed his cigarette blowing smoke into the room. But he couldn't allow the past image of himself to overtake the moment.

Jon Cam Jr. was the world's greatest undiscovered philosopher, preacher and lecturer. He was natural and spontaneous. His repertoire of religious devotion could put many a 'jack-leg' so named *called* reverend to shame with his unprompted "Father God" prayers to the Almighty. But his Biblical demeanor did not prevent him from becoming openly critical and 'blunt' on occasions if crossed. Once when he was a small boy of six sitting with his sibling around the kitchen table, Lionel, the oldest brother, criticized him for no apparent reason except to conjure up a laugh, as it was so often the case when the family gathered, "Jon Cam you look like a white-mouth mule." Jon Cam did not take to the insensitive jeer aimed at him; with the laughter of the family upon him; within a millisecond a shocking response was leveled at Lionel, "You look like a M------ F-----!" It was like the Prophet Elisha against the youths for making fun of his baldness: his comment devoured Lionel. Most young boys his age would have perhaps angrily run away from the scene to guard his feelings. Not Jon Cam. We were all young—we all sat there speechlessly, and looking at this child—one of the youngest among us, we looked at him with disbelief. Lionel sat there looking sheepishly; as we all burst out laughing at the reply.

Jon Cam candidly confessed to an unwavering dislike for teachers—envying most college degreed graduates who spoke with (what he felt) was a phony authority of the content of a senior high school history anthology. Yet, 'all' of the children, especially his own and those in the family and his grandchildren, his nieces and nephews absolutely adored Uncle Jon Cam. He could upholster a sofa; tune a car engine; sophisticated technology only occasionally baffled him and his way with words revealed an acute ability to write a descriptive paper while charming the grandchildren into behaving.

With an entrepreneurial mind set, his initiative at risk taking when he was younger, allowed him at various business ventures during the late 70s early 80s disco high-tech production age, when life was safe and the social communities were free-spirited groups dancing the night away at the clubs located up and down highway 74. His company, Illusion Entertainment Music Production, with the enormously high volume speakers provided strobe-lights music shows in the Queen City club scene and private parties. (Special calibrated strobe lights, capable of flashing up to hundreds of times per second, are used to stop the appearance of motion of rotating).

With his naturally brilliant mind like his father Jon Cam Sr., therefore it was not usually required of him a post high school course of study for most of his employment opportunities. He could *pass the test and land the job* through what he had learned via osmosis (an efficient, enjoyable and social way to learn).

He had on so many occasions easily commanded the family's attention with his wry renditions; as he spoke all were listening. He recounted, "But don't forget the time we had to block our brother, Lionel to keep him from near bout killing Karl up yonder at the ball field when Karl 'stole' Lionel (unexpectedly hit him in the jaw and ran), while we held Lionel down on the ground to keep him off of Ailey's husband." Without pausing, Cam continued, "and then I know you haven't forgotten about the time when Reynolds and Lionel got into it after coming home from Viet Nam and both of them were about 'three sheets in the wind'; they got mad about some stupid stuff, and were about to go to blows when Reynolds kept repeating to Lionel, "You think you can beat me don't you." He was out there in front of the house, in the yard, all up in Lionel's face in the Bruce Lee stance, (Cam gets up to demonstrates), making karate chops in the air with his hands talking about Kiai, Kiai, Kiai. Seeing that he had no taker and becoming a little embarrassed at himself, he decided to leave. Although it was his car they had ridden in, he then said he was going to walk back to Charlotte. He told Lionel, you take the car and he struck out down Fairley headed for Roosevelt Boulevard. Our poor Mama had to go after his a-- in the station wagon and make him get in the car!" By now everyone was in stitches with loud uncontrollable laughter while listening to Jon Cam's interpretation of the events.

Jenna, amusing hysterically and revealing a childhood attribute inherited from Lale, which she loved to flaunt as if she were boldly revealing the Esperanza— the most valued American diamond—her diastema. As she shook her head simultaneously, she divulged, loudly, "Cam you crazy! I remember how ridiculous they both looked. Mama should have kicked both of those two grown men's behinds—two supposedly respectful *War Veterans*—two doggone paratroopers!"

Topia finally stifling her belly laugh, and redirecting the conversation back to Roselyn and the matter at hand; she continued from before, "Now of all things, this "nig" she almost used the 'N' word, "this 'HEFFA' has gone and lost one of the most prestigious positions a black woman can have. I know we not only believe in taking care of our own, but we also believe in family reputation, she paused—family pride. It would be one thing to lose a job like that because of downsizing, or illness, or even insubordination; but that is indeed *NOT* the case. How can we stand up for her against those allegations of being responsible for disappearing funds under her watch? We are talking about the government here—and you know they do not play with you're a--. Y'all know she's got some serious explaining to do." She paused again to get up from her throne, to go to the kitchen sink below a window near the stove, all situated directly behind her and both were lined with plants, flatware, pots and pans, glassware; there was food in pots and pans on the stove prepared in hopes for the gathering. Her pause allowed the listeners to chew on her words.

Jon Cam, by now had smashed his cigarette butt into an ashtray. Acknowledging his sisters words courteously, "You raise some interesting points, but I don't believe the woman has done anything against the family pride. If anything, she has done tremendous things to raise it up until now. It must be *heavy;* I mean heavy, dealing with the public and with those over her in such a position. Hell, I know what a time I have in that supervisory job I have dealing with those guys under me who think they should be in my position, therefore, they look at me like: What, *you* telling *me* to do something? It can be a mess sometimes. However, I know this is all a mistake for which she will be vindicated."

"Wait a minute now, Jenna protested, "I think this family pride thing is just something we're grabbing onto to keep stirring it in a bowl. This kind of s--- happens every day to people all over the world from the highest to the lowest social standing. People make mistakes, they're going to keep making mistakes—that's why God created lawyers."

There was loud, heavy laughter and Rudy not having anything to say looked down at her glass, and seeing that the ice had melted, got up to refresh it; she joined Topia at the kitchen sink.

The other sister, the seventh child, Ailey the corrections officer, much like her father, with a witty and comical disposition on most subjects, and on most occasions had been silent up until now, whose opinion was, "The whole matter rest upon the idea of getting the family name into the papers and there would be a trial." She continued to put aside her comical stance today, today her serious concerns were, "The corporate law should deal with, the whole matter strictly." She contends, "The status of the punitive system is all but perfect; even the high authorities of the system have been found in situations less than reputable. But do they *escape* losing their freedom—most of the time *they do*—nine times out of ten because we know authoritative persons are judged by a different set of laws than the ones they judge *us* by. I hope to God Roselyn won't have to serve time. The prison system is nothing to play with—I know what that's like—locked up and isolated—it's nothing I would want any human being to endure unless she took a life, however, and even that is debatable if it's self defense; she will have to account for not having the fortitude to refuse signing a document that wasn't at first prearranged a line item review; for trusting colleagues that were not trustworthy."

"Nevertheless, what I'm afraid of is her age and her future employment prospects. How will she get the money to pay for counsel if she cannot get hired? With her name in the papers and the negative publicity about the corporation she worked for, her opportunities in that sector do not look too promising. She's a black woman and you know they can blackball her—tell companies not to hire her; make an example of her. I'm sure life for her must be extremely difficult right now, but if she has to serve time, it's going to get worse." Then she asked, "Has anyone seen her lately?"

There was no response.

At that point, there was a knock at the door. It was one of the husbands looking for his wife—the one they talked about as soon as his head turned wearing a cap that concealed his true identity. He stood there smiling widely and unsuspectingly as how they subjected him to laughter and ridicule, but their conniving, cruel remarks about him compared only to how siblings often made fun of their family member at any given time.   Seeing that it was her husband, his wife, before biding her good-bys, reminded the group in a subtle way that they had not used any of the time to talk about the care of Jon and Lale…

Her comments trailed off when Topia interrupted her. "Take some of this food, Girl. Don't leave all of this stuff here for me to eat.   Y'all eat something." Topia, now grown tired from the controversy moved herself away, went down the hall to her bedroom and closed the door.

Rudy and Cam made a plate of food then excused themselves, and one readied to leave with him who stood at the door waiting.

Ailey, becoming irritated by Topia's retiring to her bedroom, commented hurtfully, "Now you see what I'm talking about.   She didn't get tired until I had something to say.   While everyone else talked, she listened but as soon as I spoke, she has to go to bed. I'm going home, *but not* before I get some of this food. Hand me one of those paper plates."

As they all prepared to leave, and Rudy and her husband pulled out of the driveway, a van pulled up onto the driveway; it was the youngest son, Karl. He stepped out of his automobile and walked around the front of it and onto the porch.

Jenna could see his resemblance of a younger version of his father, Jon Cam Sr. Standing on the porch with a paper plate piled high with food in her hand, "Boy, you look just like Daddy. Where you been?" She asked.

But before he could answer, Ailey commanded, "Stop calling that man a boy. "Hey Karl. How you doing man?"

He chuckled, seemingly thrilled by Ailey's chastisement of Jenna, he commented, "Fine, fine. Everybody leaving?"

Jenna answered, "Yea I know I need to get on out of here. See y'all later." She walked away to her car.

Karl seeing Cam inside, he walked to the door, went inside, asked, "Where's Topia— she still up?"

"Naw." Cam replied. "She went back there to her room a good while ago. Where you headed?"

"I was coming here." He paused. "I suppose you know about Lionel's plans to get married?"

"Yea, I heard. I believe it's about time for that dude to settle his butt down don't you think?"

"Man, you know it." "Well, I suppose I'll keep on going since everybody's leaving and Topia's gone to bed." Karl said.

The two of them walk out onto the porch and close the door behind them.

8

*E*mmy called her Mom and spoke briefly to her; three years now had passed by, and she asked for Jon to wish him an eighty-seventh happy birthday. He sounded jovial when he picked up the phone and heard Emmy's voice, "Happy Birthday Daddy!" She shouted out. She asked if he or Lale needed anything and what he wanted for his birthday.

He gave the usual response, "I don't guess I need anything. But I don't suppose I can answer for your mama. If you ask her she'll tell you what she needs". He paused, "But come to think of it, I believe I know what you can bring your mama—I guess she needs a 'young stud' these days." He knew Lale was more than likely still listening on the other end of the telephone and took this opportunity to pick on her—aggravate her. Nothing made him liven up more—what he adored more than anything was to use his wit to satirize. He chuckled at his own sarcasm. He seemed to be in an improved mood having been recently released from his lengthy hospital stay.

We soon heard Lale in the background. "Emmy, you tell your daddy he's gone be in trouble with that mouth of his. A young stud is what got me in the condition I'm in now with a house full of chaps and grand chaps." And she was heard laughing at her own words.

Realizing she was speaking and listening to both of them; Emmy was enjoying hearing their camaraderie. She informed them of her intentions to drive down to see the both of them soon, probably on tomorrow if she had a chance to take care of some errands and business that she had been postponing for a week.

Jon told Emmy about the others (some of her siblings) coming tonight to celebrate his birthday. She didn't bother to go into too many details, but added, "I know I won't be there tonight because of Eddie's work schedule, but, it shouldn't take the entire morning tomorrow to take care of some business, so I will see you in the early afternoon tomorrow." She said.

Emmy's concern that the early morning hours should, she felt, allow enough time to shop at Kohl's in the university area to pick up dad's birthday gift, make the post office stop, the bank stop and a quick trip to Harris Teeter grocery store to pick up some items for dinner. And she almost forgot that she needed to go to the University to return a door key which was long-long overdue, and pick up a box of papers that were packed before the Christmas vacation, so being in the university area would be convenient.

When she hung up the telephone from talking to her parents, she called the department secretary Victoria to let her know she was coming over to the school. She neglected to tell the secretary that she needed to transact this business quickly tomorrow morning, and she was put on hold so she ended up having to call back a second time. Anyway, she finally got her on the phone and Victoria said she needed to come today because tomorrow morning won't be convenient, she would be in a meeting tomorrow morning. Emmy managed to squeeze this into her plans and then went over about 12:45. She parked in front of the school and one of the instructors was coming out. She needed to return a laptop to the department also; they hugged briefly and were told to allow the young man, William Sandos to take care of it, and he was yelling "Hey Mrs. Samuels." "Let that young man put the laptop in my trunk," she said as she went over, opened the trunk to make some room. Emmy went in and saw Victoria, picked up her box from the workroom, which was in shambles. "Jesus", Emmy whispered to herself—feeling relieved that turning in the key and picking up the box of papers meant that the University ordeal was a final step that gave closure in that part of her life. She returned home about 1:30 p.m. Feeling energetic she rearranges two living room chairs to create more space to write.

****

The next morning, in their home in the Queen City, Eddie came downstairs, got in bed with Emmy. They were feeling quite hungry. He wanted Dunkin Doughnuts. They dressed and headed for Bo Jangles— picked up grits, chicken biscuit, sausage biscuit, link sausage biscuit, then picked up a dozen doughnuts, coffee, returned home and ate at the billiard table. The food did much to pacify feelings of melancholy and heartache for the three ailing parents: Jon, Lale and yes for Eddie's mother.

Now being retired, Emmy did not have any pressing English papers to complete, so she planned to visit Jon and Lale in Morristown right around two o'clock.

Emmy helped Eddie with preparing his lunch, and before he left for work he planted a wet kiss on her lips and hugged her tightly, then he went to the garage. She peeped through the door to get a glimpse of his rear as he walked out of the garage to his truck. Eddie could be heard singing "Sha La La" by Al Green as he climbed into his Ford truck and backed out of the driveway headed in the direction of Harris Street for work.

Now that Eddie was gone, Emmy ran out the door and into the car to shop for Jon's birthday gift and for the planned visit to Morristown. She hoped to make it right around two o'clock.

It was a beautiful, crisp winter day, around sixty degrees, and she felt great! She decided to take Highway 485 pass those spacious brick homes and golf course off the highway at Lawyers Station to Idlewild Road—the scenic route to Morristown, at Secret Shortcut, and then Highway 74. As she sat at the stoplight, she whipped out the cell phone and punched in her parents' telephone number to inquire about their needs. Lale, sounding very focused and strong, answered.

"Hello."

"Hi Mom, this is your daughter Emmy."

Her mom said, "I know who you are. How you doing?"

They carried on a light-weighted conversation. She asked about her Dad. Her mom put him on the telephone—they chatted, and again she asked about their wants and their needs. They both agreed they didn't want or need anything she offered—food, medicine, etc.

She ended the conversation by telling her Mom, "I'll see you in a minute. I'm pulling onto Toby Street." She soon pulled up into the driveway; her Mom stood there in her beige silk PJ's and her white soft curls surrounded her face. She opened the storm door and peeped through focusing her eyes on Emmy as she began to crawl out of the car. She hesitated a few minutes because some boys, four or five wearing very baggy pants, long T-shirts and caps pulled down over their heads gathered in the backyard of a neighboring house across the field, at the back of her Mom's house that she could see from the side view. They had caught her attention because she had never seen them before. She was trying to decide if they looked suspicious or were they just hanging out as young people do. However, after a short while, her attention returned to the purpose for the trip, so she climbed out of the Mercedes carrying Jon's gift, locked the door and walked to the porch and into the house where Lale stood. She went in reaching for her Mom with both arms giving her a warm delicate hug.

Lale hugged back released and before locking the storm door, she stuck her head out to have a look at Emmy's car. She asked, "Is that a Brick? I love me a Buick. You know your daddy drove a Buick." She chuckled as she locked the storm door.

They exchanged these few words of the casual conversation type usually shared when she visited, and Lale was curious about the box she carried for Jon. She was told that there was a pair of PJs and socks in the box.

As they talked, Emmy's senses caught the faint whiff of an overwhelming pungent odor—then she could see what appeared to have been a pile of undigested food under the kitchen table where Jon usually sat.

She managed to ask, "Is Dad in bed."

Lale answered, "Yes, but don't wake him up."

Then his voice was heard from the bedroom "I'm here. How you doin?"

Emmy walked down the hallway a short distance, peeped into the room where he lay in bed. She stood in the doorway, and then turned on the light to make him more visible, and the whiff of dried urine on the carpet beside Dad's bed where he had turned over the plastic urinal in which he spit and urinated also became more visible.

He looked so small and withered up laying there, a wide smile flashed below his bony cheeks and a sparkling twinkle lit in his eyes that revealed his happiness and pleasure for seeing Emmy.

Seeing the box she held, he asked, "What you got there?"

Emmy walked over to his bed, handed him the gift, repeating again, "Happy belated Birthday", she placed the gift in his hand, quickly returning to the doorway.

He balanced the box on his stomach immediately unwrapped it, pulling the flannel red and navy blue pair of pajamas, matching shirt and socks from inside. "All of this is for me—well Good Lord! Thank you!" He said joyfully. "Come here Lale and look at what *we* got!" He called to his wife.

Lale came to the door, peeped in and said, "Looks like that's for you. What do you mean '*what we got?*'" She left the door to return to the living room.

They chatted as he lay there with his arms folded across his stomach and his gifts laid beside him. He inquired about Eddie, Emmy's husband "the Chief" as he was referred to. She told him the chief was 'on the job earning bucks.' Leaving him seemingly feeling lighthearted, Emmy excused herself, "I'm going up to sit with Mom, Dad." She said as she turned off the light and moved away to the living room to sit on the sofa.

In the living room Lale sat in her recliner where she watched one of those TV court shows. Judge Samantha was presiding over a domestic case for a man who wanted his wife to cook, clean, and treat him like a king.

Lale sat there talking to the television, "I'd tell him to kiss my a--. Yea, that's what I'd tell that ni----. I'd tell him to kiss my a--."

Emmy sat there amazed at the disrespect Lale first had for herself and also for her daughter. She loved her mother, but at the same time was appalled at her. She tried to think back to when she and her sisters were young, and she just didn't remember ever hearing her using that language or saying such things then to anyone. But now in her old age—eighty-five she just lets it fly—anything at anytime. Emmy felt pity for her too, that it seemed, that she was not any closer to her Lord than she apparently was. But she thought that maybe that was the way with older people. Perhaps they felt after living such a long time, they had earned the right to say exactly what they wanted. Perhaps it gave her mom a sense of some kind of power now at a weaker stage in life.

In this situation Emmy couldn't help but think about herself and felt afraid—afraid of some day being that way with her own children. She thought, God help me, I don't want to be like Mama in that pathetic way. She said, "Mama you need to be a role model for me."

But that didn't work. Lale laughed and responded the same way as before, "I'd tell him to kiss my a--." Lale seemed to be in her own isolated world— she and the people on television.

Realizing she had used the wrong approach, instead of the role model appeal, her approach should have been to tell her she was too beautiful to use such language—to lower herself to such an unattractive and unappealing level. Then again, she thought, at least this time we're not arguing about anything. She knew she should not judge her mother.

This time she had decided to make an all out effort to be agreeable no matter how much her skin crawled. In addition, as she sat there on the sofa her skin was crawling from the penetrating horrible smell of regurgitated matter coming from underneath the kitchen table, and the pungent odor of dried urine on the carpet beside Dad's bed where he had turned over the plastic urinal in which he spit and urinated. Earlier, Emmy asked for a towel or some kind of cloth to clean it up.

Lale told her, "Use the mop sitting on the deck."

Emmy responded, "I don't do mops Mama."

Lale got up, opened the back storm door and stepped out onto the deck in her bare feet to get the mop. She brought it in and showed Emmy how to use it by twisting the mop handle. She said, "This is all you have to do." Standing there in her silk pajamas, turning the mop handle. Emmy told her "Never mind." She remembered when she visited the day after Christmas, she commented on how nice the house looked. She made the mistake of saying Rudy had done such a good job.

It upset Lale, who adamantly insisted, "Rudy don't clean my house. I haven't seen Rudy in two months."

Emmy told Lale she knew that was not true because Rudy had been there twice the day before Christmas day.

Lale became irate. "That's a lie!" She insisted. "I do my own cleaning. In fact, I try to clean it every other day to try to keep up with it."

Her mind told her that Lale knew what she was saying and what she was doing — standing there and lying. Then Emmy caught herself, remembering that Lale's memory was not what it once was. She felt ashamed at her criticism.

So after sitting with her for a while, Emmy moved to the kitchen; she tore off some paper towels, wet them with warm water and sprayed some Scrubbing Bubbles on the towel to clean the floor where Jon had regurgitated; then she moved to the bedroom to clean up the spill where Jon lay in bed. She then returned to the kitchen to clean. She shook the crumbs into the sink from the placemats that were on the kitchen table, straightened the papers and cleaned the table placing the mats back; swept the floor. Lale stood over her, watching the entire interval— her every move. When Jon's placemat was removed, there seemed to be a Social Security check underneath the plastic tablecloth. Lale's watchful eyes were to make sure nothing happened to the check. Emmy thought to herself, it's not that I am not trusted. Then she remembered something that Rudy had said to her a few weeks earlier.

It's not unusual for older people to sometimes become somewhat overly protective of their possessions. So Emmy kept her tongue still and her thoughts to herself. When she finished, she returned to the couch once more and sat down.

Lale walked to the back storm door, and she made a comment about the neighborhood boys Emmy had seen earlier, about one of them being on the ground and possibly hurt. Emmy moved to the door where her mother stood, and together they watched the boys for a while; then decided that they were just being boys—just horsing around.

One of the boys walked away into the direction of the field in front of the house. The image of his rear end could be seen sticking out of his long T-shirt as he walked. "He looks like a penguin with those cloths—his pants hanging low, his shirt and sweat jacket, his cap pulled down over his head to his eyes." Emmy commented.

Lale became reminiscent of her time as a young girl. "That style is nothing new; they wore those clothes back in the day when my daddy was a boy—those old big-legged pants hanging down, long shirts and all. That ain't nothing new."

Emmy chimed in, "Didn't they call them Zuit suits?"

"I don't know. But they wore them when I was coming up."

It had begun to get dark so Emmy told Lale, "Mama I need to get up the road to Charlotte before it becomes too late."

They could hear Jon, from the bedroom, "I believe I'd like to have a Quarter Pounder. How about you Lale? Then you won't have to do anything about supper."

By now, her mom had gone and stood in the doorway to Jon's room again. "What makes you think I was planning on doing anything about supper?" She asked sarcastically.

Her dad chuckled. That was the way he had to handle most things dealing with Lale—just tries to laugh it off, or get "cussed out" royally.   "That   sounds fine, if that's what you want, I'll run right out and get them." Emmy said. She asks, "Do you want fries with your burger? Do you want a drink?"

Lale said she believed there is a whole Sprite in the refrigerator. She moved to the kitchen to check for the Sprite in the refrig.   Then, she could be heard, "There's a whole bottle of Sprite."

Emmy ran out to the car preparing to go to McDonalds, but before leaving she yelled back asking if she should go to Burger King or McDonalds?

Jon responded, "Wherever is the closest."

At that instant, before Emmy climbed into the car, Lale came to the storm door, opened it and walked out onto the porch. She called to Emmy, "When I was young, all of this use to be our playground. My mama would send us over here to play." She lifted her hand— pointed, "You see that house across the road over there? Well, that use to be June and Bobby's old house. All of this was our playground. My mama use to send us over here to play." She repeated.

****

79

Emmy thought about this poem written for Lale as she stood there on the porch.

Dedication: All for You, Mama.

MAMA YOU woke up early
In the morning
Used your brown,
Velvety hands
Made a blazing fire from cut wood
Placed under a black wash pot
Then
Filled the tin wash tub
Full of hot water
To scrub those old
Hard soiled clothes.

You scrubbed them
On a washboard
Then
Put them
In the black wash pot
Of boiling hot water
To sanitize them.

MAMA YOU carried those heavy
Wet clothes to a rinse tub
Rinsed them-rung them
You hung them on the line
To dry in the sun.
*I didn't know about
*Clean clothes then.

MAMA YOU woke up early
In the morning
Used your brown,
Velvety hands
Rung the necks
Of the chickens
Doused those feathers
With hot water.
Then
Plucked them
Cut them
Battered with flour
Fried them in lard
Saved in a tin can.

MAMA YOU put
The golden brown pieces
On the table
For us to eat.
*I didn't know about
*Chickens then.

MAMA YOU woke up
Early In the morning
Used your brown,
Velvety hands
Sewed until dawn
Even though the stone
Had been rolled
From the tomb
And it was almost time
To hide the red, yellow and pink eggs

In the tall green grass.

I was so proud
Of that dress
That you put
The finishing touches on
Just before it was time
To close the cathedral doors
At the eleven o'clock service.
Everyone said,
"Oh how pretty, Oh how fine."
*I didn't know about
*Sewing then.

MAMA YOU cut the boy's hair
While Daddy waited his turn.
YOU made their pants
Daddy waited his turn.

MAMA YOU kept
Right on smiling and humming
While you pedaled
That old Sears sewing machine
The axle turning
In locomotion
As your hands guided the seam
Needle bobbing up and down
Curving around
That bargain fabric
Bought at the five and ten.
Then
YOU adorned yourself

*And the church members said,
*"How splendid."

MAMA YOU rose the bloody spring
Right off that mouse's neck
And dumped its limp body onto the dead rat mound
That night
When we were determined
*To catch them all and keep them
*From running around the house
*Making those squeaky noises
*Biting holes in our bread.

YOU looked all polished: shined
With your face all made up
Your raspberry color lipstick
On Saturday night
When Daddy took you to the club.

MAMA YOU suddenly turned
Salt and pepper
And then silver.
*YOUR stride is slow
*Your eyes are weak.

YOU still warm
When the words
You say: **YOU REPEAT.**

YOU still soft
To the touch
*When you hold me

* And place a weak kiss
*Upon my cheek.

YOU still Mama
Before I drive away
* I turn, I see, you still standing
*On the front porch
Waving good-by—gazing across the street
At the field
Where you use to play: Hide- and-seek.

9

*L*ale's **upbringing** in Bottle Neck's neighborhood roughness in her early years could have caused irrevocable damage to her life. Throughout the segregated 'Colored' section and in school, she was famed, it was said, as a trash-talker, someone who did not hold back from voicing her opinion in spite of the fact that it usually was at someone else's expense. She behaved in a rowdy and unruly manner from the beginning as a young girl. She was brought up in a family of four children, two brothers and one sister. In her teens, because she was spoiled by a stepfather, Claude Allie, who was born in Redwood City, California, a railroad man who worked for Southern Railroads: Seaboard Coast Line that became a branch of the Southern Railway in 1940s. The Georgia, Carolina & Northern Railroad started at Morristown, NC in 1887 and built to Atlanta.

Lale's stepfather held an important job with the railroad whose job was to turn the trains around at the roundhouse before they left the station. Besides his railroad job, he bootlegged the sale of alcohol behind closed doors in the dining room of his home; and therefore, Claude Allie earned more money than most Negros of the area. In spite of the unemployment under Franklin D. Roosevelt and the Great Depression, he zoomed around town in an expensive shiny, black 1932 'rumble seat' T-Model Ford.

The family lived in a huge two-story house in Bottle Neck a part of the black ghettos, but this area did not always contain dilapidated houses and deteriorating projects, nor were all of its residents poverty-stricken. Lale wore the latest expensive Belk fashions and Sacs shoes and coats to school and to church. Like Lale, to those who lived in Bottle Neck, the ghetto was "home", a place representing authentic blackness and a feeling, enjoyment, or emotions, a by-product of rising above the strife and anguish of being black. In her neighborhood, the church was an important source of social unity and motivation; the kind of spirituality learned through the church worked as a protective factor against the callous forces of racial discrimination.

The formation of her black neighborhood was closely linked to the history of segregation in the South, either through Jim Crow laws, or as a product of social norms, collective actions taken by whites to exclude blacks from their neighborhoods.

Part of the neighborhood of her childhood was unfortunately a place where folks engaged in drinking a pint of liquor and who would not think twice about cursing you out, kicking you in the posterior and pulling out a switchblade to cut you up all simultaneously. Folks engaged in gambling and slid in and out of each other's houses as slippery as the fish they were about to fry on Friday night.

When she first laid eyes on the young and handsome Jon riding on the back of his father's wagon delivering furniture in the neighborhood, Lale was determined to have the light skinned, straight haired youthful man. Therefore, she quickly fought her way into his life—literally bullying any other female who dared to even cast an eye in his direction. She was medium height, ebony, shapely, well dressed, groomed and good-looking. Her heritage, a mixture of African American, Euro American and Blackfeet Indian--her blood ran fiery. It was believed that because she had a sharp tongue, was unafraid; did not hesitate to be outspoken, a young woman with many naturally creative skills, Jon was immediately taken by her unyielding spirit and she soon won his heart.

Although it was many years ago, Lale still had not progressed as time changed. As time changed, she found herself mothering eleven children having limited opportunity to develop the professional manifestation of any of her abilities. When she and Jon married and she gave birth to their first child, she was silently envious of Jon's matriculation as a college student at Shaw University. Then, Jon was drafted into the Army. In between having babies and working at Camp Sutton in the 40's there wasn't a chance for her to continue her education as she desired. Her mother adamantly refused to babysit her daughter's children while she went off to school. This caused great mental harm and bitterness for Lale that festered over the years.

****

On another visit, it was twelve o'clock noon and Lale sat on the front porch looking around admirably at what was before her. Her small ebony face revealed penetrating sunken hollow cheeks from time; she had become incredibly thin. Her soft white curls had a gleam about them that picked up the sunlight.

Emmy sat there beside Lale on the porch and said, "It's so nice out here. Isn't it Mama?" The love felt in her heart for her was overwhelming. The younger one ran her eyes over the older one's whole body, from her white curls down to her dark deep blue contorted feet. She was thinking of her mother when she was young, and plump, beautiful and full of fire. Now she sat here beside her very slow and very old repeating the same story. Her dementia was then becoming more and more evident.

Lale spoke, "You see that house across the road over there?" She raised her small thin wrinkled hand and pointed with a curved but not straight finger. It seemed to have almost pointed back at her self. She motioned at the direction for which she spoke.

Emmy answered, "Yes, I see it."

Lale continued, "Well June and Bobby use to live there. Yea, that use to be June and Bobby's old house." And with another breath, she repeated, "You see that house over there? That was old man R. Macomb's old house. The city had it moved over here."

Only a few moments had passed, Lale said, "You see that old house over there?" She paused, as if waiting for an answer, then continued, "Well, that use to be June and Bobby's house. Yea, June and Bobby use to live there." As the sun disappeared behind the hill and night crept upon them, Lale sat on the porch with dazed eyesight, soft white curls, folded wrinkled hands and talked to Emmy her second child about some of what she remembered of her childhood.

****

10

*S*ometimes **Lale's long term** memorization miraculously allowed her periodical recollections of stories of her life with Jon and the children that brought a delightful unexpected smile upon her face:

Daddy and the Goat

There lived a man a preacher's son in a small town of Bent Hill who everyone considered him to be very smart. Before he married and while he was in school his teachers felt that he was the smartest student that they had ever taught—making straight A's in all of his subjects. He knew physics, botany, psychology and chemistry, philosophy and theory. His teachers and his parents looked forward to the day that would come when he would take a wife. And if he and this wife would be fortunate enough to have children, they desired to see this man's children and tell them all about their smart father.

So while he was completing his undergraduate schooling, he decided to take a wife—a lovely young girl of the community who was said to have many talents. Other suitors admired this young girl, but she chose to marry the smart man who everyone admired for his brilliance. As a married couple, they were very happy because they were very much in love. They decided to live in a small house in the little town of Morristown not too far from the husband's work. The man was very smart and applied himself in every way to make a happy home for himself and his newly adored wife. His wife was proud of their lives together and so she always obeyed the laws of the marriage.

One day the couple learned that they would be blessed with an addition to the little family. They were going to have a baby. They were so happy, and the man applied his intelligence to working hard for the family so he could provide for the child's needs. And the first child was a girl—a daughter born in the first year. And so it goes, in the third year they had another daughter. And in the fifth year they had a son; and in the seventh year they had another son. And in the eighth year they had another daughter; and in the ninth year they had another daughter. And in the tenth year they had even another daughter. And in the eleventh year they had another son. And in the thirteenth year they had yet another son.

The couple soon discovered that the little house they lived in was much too small for them and all of the children because they now had nine children. So to make life better the man decided that a larger house was needed for the children. The man knew he did not have money to purchase a home. Although he was very, very smart and worked very, very hard on his job both day and night, the family was very, very poor because times were hard and money was scarce. So he rented a larger house and moved his family into it. Renting a house located on some land in the countryside owned by a landlord on Old Charlotte Road did not make the family unhappy.

Having to work harder now to pay for a larger house did not cause unhappiness either because the man relished in his glory that everyone knew him to be a very smart person. Everyone in the town knew that the man was very smart.

The landowner himself also lived on the property in a big house surrounded by a huge gate, and he was a farmer. His pigs, chickens, cows and goats roamed his land freely.

Every night after work, the man came home for supper. On this particular night his wife had prepared the family meal of chicken and dumplings and set the table for everyone to eat. Mealtime was enjoyable. The family enjoyed this time nightly because it was the coming together of all of the family members after the man had been away all during the day at his job. He was very loved and very missed when he was away. His wife knew that the chicken and dumplings warmed her husband's stomach and his spirit. As the spiritual leader of the family, the man led recitation of Bible verses before their meal to give thanks for the food, and he led family talks during mealtime. For a long time there was lots of uninterrupted laughter and happiness each night at the dinner table.

One night during their happy time at the dinner table, there was heard a loud strange noise outside. The family listened and no one could tell what the noise was or what caused it. So they listened quietly. The noise was heard several times more. The oldest children were puzzled and the young ones were very frightened. Wanting to protect his family, the man soon rose from the dinner table to have a look to see what was causing this strange noise that puzzled and frightened his family. He also wanted to see what was disturbing their joyous time at dinner.

Upon looking through the window, the man noticed that one of the landowner's goats had gotten out of the landowner's gate. He saw the goat on the back porch butting his head and his horns very hard against the back door. When an old goat gets something in his head, he won't stop for anything. That Billy goat was determined to have himself some chicken and dumplings. Apparently, he had heard talk--the church members, the boy scouts, the basketball **team** and the baseball team said they were the best chicken and dumpling in the community. The aroma floated out the window and through the air carried by the evening breeze made that goat crazy.

Wanting to chase the goat away so the children would not be frightened, and being the very, very smart man that he was, the father thought of a very, very good idea. He summons his wife and asked for her help. He told her, "Wife we must work together." Upon hearing the idea, to support her husband, the wife agreed that it was a very, very good plan indeed. And she agreed to help her husband.

In the meanwhile the man said, "You must get a pan of cold water and hand it to me." This she did, just as she was asked. Then the man said to his wife, "Wife while I hold the water, you should open the door, and I will dash the cold water on the goat's head, and he will run away leaving us to our meal." "Fine," said the wife.

So as the man stood there with the pan of cold water; the wife opened the door; the goat ran into the house.   Nine children scattered in nine different directions; the father dashed the water out onto the porch and immediately slammed the door. Thinking to himself, a great plan, and a job well done--completed through teamwork! But to his amazement and surprise there was no one at the dinner table when he turned around to face his family.   Suddenly all the man heard were the screams of his children.

The screaming of nine children even though they were very, very beautiful frightened the Billy goat very badly. So he ran for his own safety to the nearest door. And seeing the goat run to the door, the wife opened it, and out the front door the frightened goat ran forever-- never ever to return again.

Then over the next weeks, the children went to school and told the story to their teachers of how they ran. Then the schoolmates and teachers told the story to their brothers and sisters: of how the blood welted up in their heads and then in the hearts of the poor little children of the monstrous, wild goat and the pungent sweaty odor standing there at the dinner table. And the brothers and sisters told the story to their parents and friends of how the poor little children had to run for their lives, eyes bulged, and flickering to find hiding place in cabinets, under tables and beds and behind chairs. And the parents and friends told the story to their children and neighbors about how the poor little children who could have been destroyed at that moment at such a tender age if they hadn't run panic stricken for their safety with their hair standing up on the backs of their little necks with their wide eyes shining. And the children and neighbors told the story to their church members, the deacons, the ushers and the choir members of how the wild goat could have eaten alive the littlest one in the family. And the church members told their butchers and shopkeepers of how the oldest children had chased and caught the youngest ones and shielded them from harm as the wife saved the whole family. And the shopkeepers told the innkeepers and the customers—and so on and so on.

Now the story can be heard all over Morristown, on the porches and the backyards, in the stores, the churches, the shops and in the countryside that the man is married to a very, very smart wife.

Billy Goat Goes Mad: for Chicken and Dumplings

Lale's Recipe:
1 chicken cut up
1 small slice of salt pork
One large onion chopped up in medium size pieces.
Three stalks of celery chopped in medium size pieces.
Salt
Pepper
2 table spoons butter or margarine

Prepare the chicken

Wash and cook chicken in a large pot
Add 4 cups of water to the pot for the broth
Add butter, salt and pepper to taste
Add the salt pork, onion and celery to the pot.
Cook until the chicken is tender (falling off the bone)
Remove the chicken from the broth and allow chicken to cool, then remove the skin and throw away. Remove the salt pork from the pot. Throw away.
 Place the chicken back into the broth, cover and allow it to simmer while the dumplings are being made.

Prepare the dumplings

2cups self-rising flour
Pour in hot water into the flour to deactivate the baking power.
Work into a semi-dry dough. Roll dough out thinly with rolling pen, and with a knife, slice the dough into strips. When chicken is boiling again, take the strips and pull off two inches pieces of the dough and drop them into the hot boiling pot of chicken. Allow the dumplings to cook until tender. Allow it to cool. Serve warm.

****

Lillie

Once there lived a beautiful young girl in the land of Morris. She lived with her mother, two stepsisters and a stepbrother. And since the father of the other children was not her real father, she was never allowed to call him by this name, Father. This made the beautiful young lady very lonely and very unhappy. And she would sit alone in her room reading stories all by herself at night. So she vowed that someday when she married, she would have many, many children of her very own so that she could give them the love she never had.

The young lady was liked very much in school because she was very beautiful and because she could read very well. You see the more she read the better she could read. And the better she read, the more she was liked. As the young lady became older, she had two suitors who fell in love with her. And one day they both asked for her hand in marriage. Therefore, she had to choose between the two of them.

One suitor was the son of a preacher. The preacher also had many, many children and lived on lots of land. The son of a preacher would make a fine husband. The other suitor would make a fine husband also, but he had only one brother. Remembering the vow she had made to herself, the young lady choose the son of a preacher's hand in marriage because she felt that if they might be blessed with a large family, then this would make them both very happy; he wouldn't be angered by his many little children tugging at his feet.

So after they were married, during the first year the couple gave birth to their first born, a fine and healthy daughter. And the young lady, who was now a woman, cared for her daughter day and night. Soon the couple gave birth to their second born, who was also a fine and healthy daughter. And the young woman cared for the two children day and night. Then the couple gave birth to their first son who was also a fine and healthy child. And the woman took care of the three children both day and night. Then the mother gave birth to a second son who was a fine and healthy child. And she cared for the four children both day and night. Then the couple was blessed with three more daughters who were fine and healthy girls and three more sons who were just as fine and healthy. And the woman took care of the ten children both day and night. And again the couple was blessed with one final daughter who was fine and healthy baby. Now the couple had six beautiful daughters and five healthy and strong sons.

And now the young couple's hearts were very full. And the young woman wanted to give her children the stories that she read as a child so each of them would feel her love. So each night after dinner the young woman gathered the children all around her and told them the folktales, fairytales, and short stories to fill their ears and minds. She told the story of the girl with the golden hair, and the folktale of the lady who had no bread; and the fairytale of the man who slept too long each night. She continued this tradition with the children until they all grew up and they themselves took husbands and wives and were blessed with children. And to show their love they began to tell the stories to their children the way the young woman had told them.

****

"Mama Allie's Talking Dogs Fried Croakers in Peanut Oil."

A long time ago, Lale's mother, Mama Allie, lived with her grown son, Uncle Horace and his family. Uncle Horace was always telling us stories. One of his favorite stories was how much dogs love the smell of fish. He said every night at around twelve midnight just when the moon was full, dogs would meet and go on a scrounging journey in search of old smelly fish. They sniffed out areas where they knew they could find overflowing trashcans that would give them the largest, meatiest bones; bread sopped in greasy brown gravy, and drippings of syrupy sweet potato. But their very favorite cans were the ones that carried the delicious smell of fish, especially if there had been a fish fry, and the fish had been scrapped, and the head cut off and put into the cans. The cans that smelled of fish made the dogs salivate and lick the long tongue all around their mouths because dogs love fish just as much as the cats.

Mama Allie grew up in a family tradition of frying fresh fish for the family on Friday night for supper. Her mother fried fish on Friday night; her mother's mother fried fish on Friday night. Her mother's mother's mother fried fish on Friday night and so on down the line as far back as she could remember. So Mama Allie's trashcan was a favorite because this family tradition continued on Friday night. Well, these dogs would gather in packs in the neighborhood. They would decide what streets and allies to search right after sniffing out the cans at the corner store.

So like clockwork every night just about one o'clock in the am a pack of ten to twelve dogs with their leader, the dog with the most brains, would attack and turn over Mama Allie's trashcan scattering the garbage all over the alley in back of the house.

You see Uncle Horace worked hard on his job at Southern railroad all day and needed his sleep at night. And each time the dogs turned over the garbage while scrounging around looking for something smelly and something good to eat, it was his job to get up very, very early the next morning to clean up the trash before going off to work.

So each Saturday morning when Mama Allie got up very early to make breakfast of left over fish, grits and biscuits she looked out of the kitchen window overlooking the alley just before putting the coffee on the stove, she could see the overturned cans from the night before. She called upon Uncle Horace to clean the mess up.

One day Uncle Horace became tired of his sleep getting interrupted by having to get up extra early to clean up the mess made by the dogs the night before. So he decided to do something about the dogs turning over Mama Allie's garbage can. He thought and thought to himself about what to do. Finally he thought, "If I put the can in the old barn behind the house then the dogs won't be able to find it anymore. And this way I can get some sleep, and I won't have to clean up the garbage in the alley anymore."

Uncle Horace felt that he had a good idea. So he went to talk to Mama Allie about it. She asked him, "Son do you think it will work? I sure do want you to get your rest because you work so hard. Why don't you try it and see?"

Uncle Horace told his mother, "All right then I will." You see it was Friday and they were going to eat fish for supper.

So on Friday night after supper Uncle Horace closed the lid very tightly on the can and put it in the barn and locked the barn door. He later went to bed. In the meanwhile, the dogs gathered as they usually did preparing to go looking for food. After they checked all of the cans at the local stores they rounded the corner to the alley where Mama Allie and Uncle Horace lived. But to their surprise when they arrived they could smell the delicious fish that made their mouths water, but there was no garbage can. They huddled and the group decided that the dog with the most brains would ask the question. So he begins, "Roo, roo, roo-roo-roo-roo-roo." Roo, roo, roo-roo-roo-roo-roo?" There was no response. So he asked again. "Who, who, who moved that garbage can?" This time when the dog with the most brains didn't get an answer, he began to bark louder because he knew that the other dogs wanted to know what had happen to that garbage can with the fish in it. So he demanded "Roo, roo, roo-roo-roo-roo-roo?" (Who, who, who moved that garbage can)?"

In the meanwhile Uncle Horace was awakened by the commotion. To scare the dogs away, he loaded his old shotgun, opened a window and shot into the air making a loud Boom! This gave the pack of dogs a good scare. And the dog with the most brains told the other frightened dogs as he led the trembling pack down the alley and away from the house without looking back, "I KNOW NOW! I KNOW NOW!"

Now Uncle Horace goes off to work fully fed and well rested with plenty of sleep. And the dogs never returned to search for food in the alley behind Mama Allie's house again.

Mama Allie's Talking Dogs Fried Croakers in Peanut Oil © 2003: Connie Williams

Mama Allie's Talking Dogs Fried Croakers in Peanut Oil
4-medium size Croakers (heads removed cleaned and split open)
Yellow corn meal
1 egg
Salt and black pepper
3 cups Peanut Oil

Note* Mama Allie used Crisco to fry her fish. I use Peanut Oil for a crispier taste. I believe she would be pleased.

Heat the peanut oil in a deep fryer. Wash and drain the water from the fish. Beat the egg and dip the fish into the batter. Add salt and pepper to taste. Cover the fish in the corn meal and fry until golden brown in the hot peanut oil. Serve hot.

11

"***M**ama is going shopping* but she has to cuss Daddy out first."   Topia was talking on the telephone to Emmy. It was now one thirty and Topia had come to pick Lale up to take her to Food Lion. She had seen after her, removing the soiled, blood stained clothes she wore. She had seen after her, bathing and steadying her while she put on a set of fresh clean clothes, combed her hair for her.   As she sat on the sofa talking to Emmy and waiting for Lale to get her purse, she waited as she watched Lale walk in and out from room to room like she had lost something.

Topia briefly paused for a moment, her conversation with Emmy to ask, "Mama, are you looking for something?"

Lale answered, "I'm trying to decide when to cuss your daddy out. He ain't good for a doggone thing but eating, sleeping and defecating."

Jon sat in his chair in the kitchen beside the kitchen table clutching his hands with his arthritic fingers intertwined, his head lowered; he sat in a napping state. He raised his head and opened his eyes when he heard Lale. He said, "You didn't think like that when you *were* trying to get your hands on me over yonder with your dress over your head. You must have thought I was worth something then. If I'd known then what I know now I'd be running till **yet!**"

Lale came from the living room taking little baby like steps, moving as slowly as cold thick molasses sliding down the side of a jar, she stood directly in front of him, "Don't mess around and get your butt kicked. If you know what's good for you, you had better keep your doggone mouth shut. If you didn't want my hands on you, why didn't you keep your raggedy behind on the other side of town over there on Bent Hill where you belonged?"

Jon complained, "I wish you would stop coming over here and getting in front of me and standing on top of my feet. I thought you had to go to the grocery store."

Topia ends her conversation with Emmy, hangs up the telephone, she reminds Lale of what they were supposed to be doing. "Mama are you about ready to go to the store? I do have some things I need to do at home, so you need to come on if you want to go because I'm going to the car."

Lale turned her attention to what Topia has said, and walked away from the kitchen where she had been standing in front of Jon, "I could have been ready, if your daddy would stop agitating me. That's all he knows how to do is keep something going." She picked up her purse from the coffee table, "I'm ready—let's go."

The ride to the grocery store was a short one. Lale rode, her legs straddled, purse in between them, continuously putting her hand in and out of it searching and picking through it. At a point when her hand was out, the car stopped at a stop light causing it to tumble over finally to the car floor and the contents spilled out at her feet. Topia, trying desperately not to scream, simply turned on the radio, turning the knob to locate a station while she waited for the light to change. Lale leaned forward in an attempt to gather up her purse and its contents. While the car stopped, she fumbled around with her hand on the floor picking up her loose coins, her hair comb, her wallet, lipstick, lotion, store coupons, her house keys and a pack of Juicy Fruit chewing gum. But before she could put them all back, the light changed.

As Topia started the car again, she said, "Don't worry about that, we'll take care of it when I get parked at the store."

Lale picked up the purse securing it on her lap with her elbows over it so it would not fall again. Still securing her purse, she took her hands, started to unwrap a stick of gum from all sides. She turned it over on all sides. The paper seemed to be stuck to the gum so she picked, and picked and picked at it with child like effort finally opening one end of it enough to tear a small piece apart and put it into her mouth—she began to chew making smacking sounds, while picking at the paper on the rest of the gum.

Topia was glad the radio played "Baby I'm Yours." The song allowed her to block out Lale's smacking sounds with thoughts that drifted to a more pleasant time when she traveled to New York to one of her old high school mate's birthday party. She thought of how she wished her friend were still alive, how they had so much fun together—when they danced the "Watusi," the " Boogaloo" and the "Slide" practically all night while sipping on Gin and juice. When the sun came up, they went out to breakfast to eat flapjacks and drink piping hot coffee at the corner I-Hop. Not like now when all she does is work, go to church on Sunday and sometimes out to dinner with a BFF, and take care of her parents and then back to work again. She almost said it aloud, "I haven't been to a good party in years." As she pulled into the Food Lion parking lot, she said quietly to herself, "Thank God."

"You say something?" Lale asked. But before there was any response, she continued "You mean we're here already?"

"Yea, we're here." Topia pulled the car into a parking space, rolled the window up and got out, walked around to Lale's side and opened the door.

"I got to pick up my stuff off the floor." Lale leaned forward to pick up her paraphernalia from the floor.

But Topia gathered up the items quickly, grabbed Lale's purse shoving them inside. "Here!" She said handing her the purse; she took Lale by the arm and helped her out of the car, rolled up the window, closed and locked the door. They walked into Food Lion.

"It's cold in here, and I didn't wear a sweater. Lale said.

By now, Topia noticed that the watch on her arm said two fifteen. As she pushed the shopping cart though the grocery store, which carried Lale's jar of Jiffy creamy peanut butter and loaf of bread, she watched her meander, aimlessly, like a lost child—up then down, and in and then out of isles, occasionally picking up items, holding them closely up to her eyes, and putting them down on the shelf again, finally stopping at the soap, detergent and bleach section. "Mama you are out of washing powder and soap?"

Lale paused for a moment, then, she said, "Yea, but you know I don't buy this cheap stuff. It won't get a doggone thing clean. My mama always used Tide, and I always buy Tide." She walked over and pointed to a box of Tide on the shelf. "Get one of these."

Topia took a box from the shelf, put it into the cart and they moved on pass the detergent section to the soft drinks and stopped. Lale continued, "When I washed clothes for Old Lady Whitt, you know she didn't use *no* bleach. She didn't have to because Tide is strong enough to clean anything. Old Lady Whitt sure was good to me. Whenever I needed to be off for any of you chaps, she didn't mind as long as I did the laundry. She would say, Lale, be sure to wash the bed linen. Shucks, she changed the bed bout every other day. I washed those sheets and pillowcases and hung them on the line in that morning sun—her sheets and pillowcases were as white as snow and smelled as fresh as spring rain. Get your daddy a Dr. Pepper. You know he's got to have that when he eats his peanut butter sandwich."

Topia pulled a two- liter bottle of Dr. Pepper from the shelf and put it into the cart.   Lale   began again as if she had not spoken these words before, "You know when I washed clothes for Old Lady Whitt, she didn't use *no* bleach. She didn't have to because Tide is strong enough to clean any doggone thing. Old Lady Whitt sure was good to me. Whenever I needed to be off for any of you chaps, she didn't mind as long as I did the laundry. She would say, Lale, be sure to wash the bed linen. Shucks, she changed the bed bout every other day. I washed those sheets and pillowcases and hung them on the line in the morning sun..."

As Lale' talked, Topia guided the grocery cart to the meat section and chose a pack of ground hamburger and put it into the cart, then pushed it to the checkout counter, paid for the items, watched the lady at the register bag the groceries, place them in the cart, and the two of them left the store.

In the car on the way home, Lale asked, "Did we get some tooth paste? We're almost out of tooth paste."

Topia said forcefully, "Mama, we went right pass the tooth paste isle; you didn't say a thing about getting tooth paste. We can go back –oh, I'll pick some up for you later while I'm out."

Lale started again, "Your daddy has to have the stuff for his dentures, but I like the stuff with the whitening in it—you know that Arm and Hammer. That's the best tooth paste in the world. I can't just use any kind of tooth paste on my teeth." Lale took a breath and continued, "You know this section of town sure has changed. I remember when I was a girl there wasn't a single store, restaurant or nothing on this street. Back then, they called it Charlotte road. I remember my daddy had a hog pen over here with Chester Whites, that's what he said they were—Chester Whites; and my brother, Horace, would have to walk over here every afternoon with a bucket of slop to slop the hogs. Now, you can't hardly get nowhere round here on this road—in or out on it." She laughed softly in amusement of herself; then dug deeply into her pocket book and pulled out a stick of her Juicy Fruit and started to pick at the wrapper again—opening one and shoving it into her mouth as if she needed to reward herself for her analysis. In between smacking on her gum, she repeated her scrutiny as if Topia had not heard it, "I remember when there wasn't *nothing* on this street. They called it a road back then..."

In her mind, Topia just needed to drive Lale home, put the groceries away and get away from her and Jon for a while. She thought of her own age and how sometimes simple things unnerved her. She just couldn't take it like she could have ten years ago. She wanted this trip to the store over. She needed some peace of mind.

12

*R*udy unlocked the storm door with her key and went inside. As she crossed the living room, she did not see Jon in his recliner or on his high chair where he usually sat at the kitchen table, especially during the early hours of the day, the one Emmy had given him on the last Christmas.

Between the refrigerator and the kitchen cabinets, she could see his feet sticking out like a rag doll that someone has forgotten, tossed aside and left. Without hesitation Rudy ran to the kitchen where Jon lay on the floor in a pool of urine— his legs with the arthritic knees sprawled open. When she leaned over him, the overwhelming stench penetrated her nostrils and caused her to gag; she instantly covered her mouth tightly with her hands. Jon's eyes were not moving, stayed fixed onto the ceiling; his walker lay on the floor beside him.

Oh God, this does not look good, she thought. She called to him desperately, "Daddy!—Daddy!" Although his chest did move up and down she placed the back of her hand close to his nostrils, she therefore could feel a faint breath— that he was indeed breathing. She slapped his face lightly two-three times with her fingertips on each of his sunken cheeks. There was no response. Lale was not around, so Rudy called to her, "Mama, Mama!" Lale did not answer. "Oh my God!" She stood. Her purse still hung from her shoulder; she searched around the content inside, found and pulled out her cell phone with trembling fingers, she hastily punched in the numbers 911.

A lady answering the call said, "Yes, 911, what is the emergency."

Rudy responded in a high-pitched, frightened, penetrating voice, "It's my daddy; he's lying on the floor and not responding to his name. He's eighty-seven years old. Please hurry to 827 L'rac Street."

"Mam, who are you?" asked the voice on the other end.

Rudy answered, "I'm his daughter, Rudy Tillman."

"Do you know how long he's been lying there like this?"

"No I found him like this when I came in about five minutes ago."

"Stay calm and stay with him, we're going to send help right away."

Rudy thanked the operator, placed her cell phone and her purse on the kitchen counter, she simultaneously called out to Lale mechanically, and then without thinking, she picked up her phone again to dial Topia's number. As she kneeled over Jon again, she heard Lale's slowly moving footsteps coming down the hallway, across the living room and into the kitchen.   "What's wrong with your daddy?" She asked moving closer to him now.

"I don't know, I found him like this when I came in. Do you have any idea how long he's been laying here, Mama?" Before Lale could answer, Topia was on the line.

"Hello." Topia said.

"It's Daddy, he's here on the floor in the kitchen, Topia, his eyes are fixed onto the ceiling and he's not answering when I call his name."

Without hesitation, Topia says, "I'll be right there. Rudy, have you called an ambulance?"

"Sure." The two both hung up their telephones.

By now, Rudy could hear a siren in the distance.

****

Floating in dreams of opportunities gone by, a lost soldier of World War II, Jon's unconscious state gave way to witty and sometimes sharp condemnations often revealed in an attitude of twenty-first century survival. Otherwise, he often felt eaten alive in his own skin. Lying again between the sheets of the secured-railed bed with the seep-seep-seep of medicine, which hung from a bag, and trickled into his left arm, he dreamed peacefully. It did not matter that he was a lost soldier of World War II, as long as he had some peace—

peace from the every-day struggle of life—the every-day struggle with pain—the every-day struggle with getting up in the morning, and trying to make it through the day. The simple events so often taken for granted when "the bloom is still on the rose, and there is brilliance in the meadow."

He lay there in the hospital bed with his children once again lined up on each side of it as his dreams took him far, far from them, away to springs of yesterday and roses that smelled as sweet as sugar tasted contrasted against the fumes of war blast and steely army ammunition.

His telephone call reached Lale, and she answered with enthusiasm and delight, "Hello Jon." She said. "Hey baby, did you get your ticket for the noon train?" Jon asked. "I sure did." Lale answered with excitement in her voice. "And I'll be arriving tomorrow at twelve thirty. I can hardly wait to see you."

It had been a whirlwind of a courtship and marriage and then an army life for Jon, leaving for two years his young wife and first-born child back in the states. His heart was overwhelmed with the events of his life—which were nothing like what he had expected, but he had to play the hand he had been dealt.

****

He remembered the train pulled up to the depot and came to a screeching halt; Lale stepped off into the chilly October weather wearing her beige and black P-coat with matching hat. Jon stood there in brown Army fatigues waiting anxiously and waving his hand vigorously as she ran to his extended open arms.

It was Friday, 1943; Aberdeen was the testing grounds for army war materials and ammunition. Jon's troop was about to be sent to Tennessee early Monday morning and later to the California Army Base, a depot for those about to be deployed over sea— first to New Zealand then to Australia and finally to the Philippine Islands.

Maryland, like North Carolina, on the Atlantic coast was as separated as pouring grease into water— with its white and colored sections.

From the train station, the couple hailed a taxicab, which took them to the colored side to eat dinner at Sonny's smoking ribs and juke joint where they ate ribs and potato salad, sipped on Kentucky Bourbon with Coke and danced the night away to Stormy Weather by Lena Horne and Cab Calloway tunes whispering their love and loyalty for each other. His dream allowed him to remember how he sniffed her sweet perfumery, talcum smell when he held her close to his chest. The warmth of her breath on his neck as they danced had made him hold on to her tightly. And, in the wee hours of Saturday morning, they strolled along holding hand-in-hand into the park where they settled onto a bench and kissed each other gently—finally she was cuddling her body close to his, as they became one under a tree and the stars. He was lost in her clutches—lost in her warmth—lost in her splendor. She was young; she was slim with long slender-graceful arms encircling him, and his desire for her was like nothing he had ever known before. Her beauty astounded him whenever he gazed into her eyes—eyes that he knew could be fiery, but at times like this were the softest he had ever seen. In his dream, a whimper flowed from her lips and into his ear like the fluid flowing—seeping into his arm and he was back again standing at the train depot waving her good-by.

****

He moved his legs in the bed and he heard the faint words of Lale.

"You trying to leave me Old Man?"

He opened his eyes slowly. At first he was not sure if the words were in his dream or if they were in the present—the here and now. Then he heard her voice again. At first, his vision was not clear. He heard her ask,

"Are you awake, Jon?"

He turned his head to focus his eyes upon her. "I'm awake." He replied weakly.

She leaned down, kissed his forehead with a quick peck of her lips and repeated, "I believe you're trying to leave me."

Her kiss reminded him of SWAK (Sealed with a Kiss) that she always wrote at the end of her letters to him. Finally he answered her, "Naw, naw, I'm not trying to do that."

He could see four of his children who stood there at Lale's side. They too wanted to know how he was doing.

His doctor informed Rudy that Jon had a touch of pneumonia, and was put on some antibiotics. Dr. Bailey reported that following his first three days at Union Memorial, Jon would need to spend a short period in the convalescent unit at Morristown Health facility before going home.

****

During his convalescence events were progressing as expected, but then one night while Jon lay in bed asleep, when all of his children and Lale had gone home, a fire occurred in the wardrobe in his room at the Morristown Health facility that turned into a big investigation scene involving the Health authorities, the Morristown Police and the Morristown Fire Department. Jon had to be instantly moved to a new room, and although he was not injured, obviously the family was called to a meeting about the unexpected and unfortunate incident.

The family members were quite displeased and wanted some explanation about the probability of him losing his life caused by smoke inhalation or something worse, losing his life by fire. Obviously, Jon being his age with impaired agility, if caught in a fire it could be detrimental. Jon's children wanted to know why this area wasn't being monitored. Who was responsible?

It was later determined that it seemed to be just an "unexplainable occurrence." And the nurses, doctors, and facility managers were most apologetic.

Rudy and Topia concluded that the health facility did not want the family to bring any type of legal suit against them in the light that no one was hurt.

When the meeting was concluded, and behind closed doors, 'Baby Girl' predicted, "Daddy might have been up to his old habits—sneaking around and trying to smoke a cigarette and discovered they were possibly about to "bust him" for smoking in the facility and therefore thought he had put the cigarette out before throwing it into the wardrobe right before his room was about to be monitored. Y'all know how Daddy is when it comes to smoking. He's lied on me so many times, even when I wasn't thinking about a cigarette— sometimes when I was nowhere around."

A few days later, the family members and Jon's Power of Attorney were asked to sign a certified document that released the doctors, nurses and staff of any wrong doings and that no charges against them or the facility would be filed, and therefore, the matter was dropped. Jon was soon released and he went home to Lale…

13

*T*he telephone rang, Emmy could see that it was Reynolds on the line when she flipped open her cell phone to check the number. She answered, "Hello."

There was a hesitation. Then Reynolds spoke. "I have something I need to tell you."

Emmy, not sure of what was being said asked, "I'm sorry, what did you say?"

"I have something to share with you." Reynolds changes his words this time.

Emmy was in bed when the call came in. Now having gotten out of bed and listening tentatively, she asked, "Should I be sitting down?"

Reynolds replied, "No, you're okay." He continued as Emmy listened. "I might be leaving The Queen City—relocating." There was another pause as Emmy listened.

"Well, where are you going?"

"I have a good chance to be hired at a new company in Phoenix."

Interrupting him, "I beg your pardon?" Emmy said.

"I had a good interview and I stand a chance of heading this new department at a company's— technology sales department. I'm supposed to fly out there next week to meet the team and you know get a feel for what's going on."

He explains, "The Phoenix Technical Testing Base (PTTB) is a company formed to promote the top standard in freeway invention resources technology and challenges through certified technicians.

PTTB certification emphasizes a hands-on approach, that is, technicians must satisfactorily perform test methods as well as pass a written exam to receive certification. The organization is represented by members from the Phoenix Department of Transportation (PDOT), highway contractors, and materials suppliers, materials testing laboratories, Phoenix Rock Products Association (PRPA), and Associated General Supplier (AGS)."

Emmy listened without interruptions but her mind took off into several different directions.

Almost without taking a breath, Reynolds continued, "They have an official cite here in North Carolina too. The Network Systems program in the

School of Testing Base at PTTB Technical Base can help students develop knowledge and skills that they can use to perform tasks associated with maintaining different computer network systems. Topics in the curriculum, explored through classroom theory and practical applications in a laboratory environment, include network operating systems and network systems design and implementation. If you have strong problem-solving, analytical and communication skills, the study of network systems administration may fit your skills and interests.

The program can help graduates pursue careers in a variety of entry-level positions in various fields involving network systems administration, such as system/network administrator, broadband technician, cable installation technician, and computer consultant and computer support specialist."

Emmy jumped in to interrupt, "Are you sure you want to move so far away from the rest of us?"

"Well I think the change might be good for me."

And before Emmy could ask about her sister-in-law, Reynolds wife, he assured her that he did not really want to debate the subject.

"Most campus-based programs blend traditional academic content with applied learning concepts, devoting significant time to practical study in a lab environment. Advisory committees, comprised of representatives from local businesses and employers, help each PTTB Technical Basse periodically assess and update curricula, equipment and laboratory design."

Finally, Emmy manages to get a question in, "And what *is* Deloris saying about all of this? You know, the probability for having to start all over again in a new location?"

"Well she's not going. She plans to stay here and keep her job. And I'll just fly home on most weekends."

"Are you **sure** you've thoroughly thought this through—I mean, it seems like it's going to be a stressful situation. Did you say you'll locate to Phoenix or Tucson?"

"Let me call you back; I need to take this call that's coming in." Reynolds hung up.

Emmy heard the dial tone on her telephone. She couldn't help but wonder had Reynolds gone to see Jon; she resisted the attempt to call him back to ask.

14

*L*ale's illness at age eighty-seven: The bloodstains on the nightgown she wore and on her pillar on the bed each morning; the vacant stare in her eyes and the frailness of her limbs were an indication of the severity of her illness. It was soon arranged that the nurses from Hospice would arrive three times a week to clean her breast and apply new bandages.

Meals on Wheels dropped off food for the two of them. Morristown County Meals on Wheels plans, supplies, and delivers nutritious and appealing meals, with the help of volunteers, to the homebound who are physically or mentally unable to shop for and/or prepare meals for themselves. Neither Jon nor Lale were able to perform the basic necessary and personal hygiene for themselves—things they absolutely needed, things they absolutely could not exist without, like baths, getting dressed, brushing their teeth, manicuring their nails and toenails, or shampooing their own hair. The health necessities one takes for granted, the aspects of living not thought about because it habitual. The preservation of their health totally became the responsibilities needed to be given over to others. Now, at age eighty-seven and eighty-nine, their needs were numerous.

None of the siblings were able to move into the house with their belongings for the long-agreed upon daily commitment that needed to last until the end of their days.

Topia said to the family, "We have to take things on a day to day—week to week basis regularly overseeing to their needs which are many."

The shopping, the house cleaning, the laundry, doctor's visits, schedules of administering the taking of medicines, the banking, the paying the bills, monitoring the mail, the phone calls; their needs took precedence over most occurrences. Jon's side of the table became overcrowded with bottles of pills and liquid medicines and schedules of when to take what—and what not to mix with what.

Boxes lined the refrigerator, the kitchen counter and the stove with food dropped off by Meals On Wheels, loving family members and caring neighbors that sometimes began to smell and attracted the crawling pest—roaches and ants. Therefore a regular extermination plan was expedited mostly by Rudy. Regular plans-work schedules sometimes had to be altered.

Their needs intensify both during the early hours as well as into the late night. Without professional maid service, the house was literally in shambles. It became necessary to enlist the assistance of as many family members who were willing to help.

This is when they all discovered the total strength in family unity; there was the need to have impromptu meetings as the needs arose; consequently, there was the need for scheduled, and planned—sit down, discuss, and organize meetings, literally recorded meetings of who should do what and when meetings. There was heavy reliance upon modern technology—telephoning and texting. Most just jumped in and did what was instinctively necessary. When the duties and tasks overlapped, they came together hugged and celebrated what had been accomplished for Jon and Lale.

After cleaning sometimes, they rubbed their father's head and neck with alcohol to make him feel better, soaked his curled fingers in soapy water. Rudy cut his hair, clipped his fingernails, and poured him something good to drink—usually Doctor Pepper. Lale slept frequently, so usually when they were doting on Jon, Lale was napping.

Rudy washed and straightened Lale's hair, on a routine basis, saw that she was bathed and dressed in some warm clean and comfortable clothes, and elevated and rubbed her feet. On days when the nurses were not scheduled to come to the house, Rudy managed to administer Lale's treatments: clean the blood from her mom's breast, apply a prescribed antibacterial ointment and bandage her wounds.

Topia and Rudy saw to it that doctor visits scheduled were met.

During their regular "rounds" of the day, and usually before noon, Jenna and her husband Jude, Ailey and her husband sped up in their automobiles and jumped out with breakfast, sometimes homemade, and sometimes from McDonalds or Hardies. On some days of the week they carted in early dinners brought right off the hot burner of the stove. Their intentions were to help Jon get his proper nourishment, get his bath, get dressed—whatever and where ever they could assist.

15

*S*trong will Lale on occasions flashed back to times when she could think productively and could run and control her own home. Poor Lale!

In spite of their daily discord though, at night in their bed when they began to sleep together again in the same room and in the same bed, Jon cradled Lale in his thin weak arms as they fell silently asleep. When he awoke in the morning, he found his small but secret stash of Viagra and with his arthritic fingers tugged at the opening of her nightgown. After all the years, Lale still never refused him.

And as daylight turned into dusk, they often reached across to each other, and held hands as an expression of their love for each other, as they sat at night in their separate recliners watching television in the living room of their home.

Treatment of each other still remained the same. Their arguments were only a way to continue to communicate in their own special way. They knew their love for each other ran so inherently deep.

At age 75
Lale wrote in her memoirs:
I went into my little bathroom
To shed a tear.
But I was frightened
When I scared a mouse
Hiding in the corner
That wanted to get out
Just as badly as I did.

At age 87 Lale says:
I didn't bother anyone
And no one
Bothered me.

At age 89 Jon says:
Things will come and go
As they will.

16

*F*inances were not a great issue. Jon and Lale both labored all of their lives for a good forty plus years, so they had their incomes, Social Security and Pensions, Veteran's benefits. As the caregiver the legal functions of stepping in and handling the finances, the taxes, medical decisions and actions on behalf of and in the best interest of the couple, Rudy was appointed the Power of Attorney.

Situations involving money was sometimes an issue concerning the elderly parents. Knowing of the steady income and their venerability to withstand the effects of a *get-over environment,* their inability to sometimes make rational decisions which may cause them to refuse passing out handouts to some relatives whose intentions were   to take advantage of the situation—this had to be dealt with. These incidents were apparent and especially manifested at night when the siblings where gone, and some distant relative or some neighborhood stranger appeared, when there was no one from the immediate family to monitor and oversee what was transpiring. As soon as this was discovered, Rudy and Topia quickly "nipped these incidents in the bud." Regrettably, however necessarily they sternly informed certain individuals they could not enter the home unless one of the siblings was present. Jon and Lale were instructed to keep the doors locked.

Telephone   calls   from   scammers   DRUG DEALERS that contact the elderly daily by telephone with the intentions of taking advantage of their vulnerability. Mortgage companies were calling Jon offering supposedly opportunities to refinance the home, and therefore trying to get him to agree to schedule meetings in his home without supervision. They promised instant money to do any needed repairs or add on; companies offered money to go on extended cruises with other senior citizens of their peers, supposedly to places one should see in a lifetime like the Bermudas, the Caribbean, Fiji Islands and Hawaii with dancing girls in hula skirts. The scammers' method was to convince the elderly couple to believe that they haven't lived until they see these places and how they guaranteed a once-in-a-life time experience. Of course alluding to "these experiences one should have before death."

Veteran donation organizations called, Homeless organizations   called,   Fire   Department,   the   Police

Department called all soliciting for donations over the telephone every day about the same time of the day.

Of course Jon with his brilliant mind felt he could handle these situations, which, indeed he could not handle the shrewdness of twenty-first century telecommunication solicitation and trickery.

On numerous occasions it was necessary for Rudy to undo some of Jon's mistaken acts of financial deeds posed as deeds done in good faith by the caller's attempt to take advantage of the elderly.

Then Jon had to be delicately warned by Topia and Rudy, "Do not talk to anyone trying to sell you something over the telephone no matter how nice it sounds. And if one of them knocks on the door, do not allow them entrance under any circumstances."

As a part of their continued survival and human needs, of course they desired to answer the telephone— of course they wanted to talk to the relatives—their children, grandchildren, great-grandchildren that many times were calling. These desires for both Jon and Lale, as well as for the calling relatives were evidently an indication to reveal that the couple was still vibrant.

****

Grandchildren and great-grandchildren's genuine concerns through their visits and telephone calls to Jon and Lale from around the globe, locally; ones from Morristown, Charlotte, Huntersville, Lincolnton, and long distance, Florida, New York, New Jersey, California, Michigan, etc. revealed how much these two were loved and thought of.

It was difficult to keep up with the outpouring of expressions of appreciation and apprehension they had for the **CORNERSTONES** of the family. The extended generations knew in their hearts that there would be a great void and a great loss. They wondered 'how the family would hold together without them.'

They adored being there in the house—their home where they spent their days and nights together. The environment was ornamented with the family photos, the books, Lale's pots and pans that she must have used to cook a thousand chicken and dumpling meals, with Lale's crystal, especially her colorful crocheted pieces and her knitted afghan patterns of themes and designs that laid on the back of the sofa, that she spent so much thought and energy creating of which she was so proud.

On occasions Lale would give one of her afghans as a gift, or give an old photograph that she wanted a child to have, especially, just from her hands to theirs, because *IT WAS ALL THAT SHE HAD TO GIVE THEM*, vowing them to not disclose the act of the gift to the other siblings because of her love and she did not want to create sibling rivalry among them. She would say, "Now don't tell the others." Therefore, her gift became sacred between her, and that child, in other words, between them and the Lord.

The twelve children, the thirty three grandchildren and twenty great-grand's were so accustomed to "going to their Mama's, Daddy's Grandma's and Grandpa's home whenever they desired to just see them—sit and talk to them whenever they were in the neighborhood. They were never refused by Jon and Lale. The house had always been as Lale would say "**FULL OF CHAPS.**"

****

Compassion for them in the hearts of everyone in the family, community, church, and medical professions became more pronounced because it was unfortunately realized that their times were coming near.

Prayers of the Saints for them at Mount Olive, the Ebenezer Baptist Church and bulletin, Friendship Baptist Church, and the Missionary Circle were resounded in the congregations and up to heaven.

Restaurants, churches, relatives and well wishers in Morristown unbelievable consistently gave provisions like anyone could have imagined could be done: fried chicken, green salad, macaroni and cheese, green beans, desserts, tea and bread all in the ever loving name of the Lord.

17

*L*ale's state of mind worsened and the body weakened. Then she was found by Topia unresponsive and lying on the floor with Jon Cam Sr. standing helplessly over her. His demeanor seemingly to appear the way his behavior was the many times he stood over her during childbirth for their twelve babies about to come into the world.

"Mama, Mama, can you hear me? Mama, can you hear me?" Topia called to Lale.

The ambulance was there in a flash and Lale was taken to Union Memorial Hospital.

Rudy again made the calls to notify her siblings about Lale's condition.

Rudy refused to go home. Her face clearly wore expressions of solemn panic and deterioration. But she slept in a chair beside her mama at night at the hospital. Her soul would not allow her to leave Lale alone.

****

Topia began to break down. Lale's condition took its toll on the family, but it especially affected the oldest when the doctor informed them of Lale's terminal illness; it was discovered that she would not be returning home to her husband Jon's side.

Topia, being a widow of many years and childless, needed something, someone to fill the void. She already collected stuff—all kinds of stuff—small projects to tinker with that sometimes helped occupy her mind, when she wasn't on her job at the Morristown school system, or when she wasn't helping Jon and Lale; when at night she was at home and lonely. But then she needed a ticking-beating heart, a sound, a response that stuff, ceramic object, plastic plants—stuff cannot provide. There is no life in inanimate objects—they are not warm, cannot give sound, and cannot show love.

Animals, she decided, could temporarily perhaps fill that void. Cats became her companion: yellow striped ones with green eyes, a large bold black tomcat that petrified most of the family members, three small kittens, a pair of male and one female from the sane litter; a black and white kitten that spent most of the time in Topia's bed. One gray Siamese cat that was vocal and demanding, capable of demonstrating his wants in a range from mews to loud harsh calls, also curious, affectionate and muscular was also her favorite.

The Siamese cat uttered sounds like human baby cries. Emmy heard it for herself when she stood in the living room of the duplex and listened to the cat make sounds that communicated to Topia.

Topia responded back, "What's the matter Baby?" calling it by a name she had given to the cat. Then the cat made some mewing sounds when Topia asked, "Where are you?" And the cat responded back. Now that was something Emmy didn't know about cats.

Topia said, "Baby loved to be around its favorite people and will share your pillow at bedtime." This Siamese cat was especially appealing to Topia, supposedly because she never had children of her own.

As if the nine cats she already had weren't too much in the first place, then the whole situation totally got out of hand, because as all animals will do, the cats reproduced. It progressed to cats crawling into the window, crawling out of the hole they tore in the screen to escape to the woods to answer the animal mating call and return to give birth to another feline.

Before long there were a house and yard full of cats in the kitchen, the bedroom, on the kitchen counters, tables, in chairs. Cat food was everywhere, and so were cat feces causing the small duplex Topia lived in to stink to high heavens. But still they were something breathing and moving that greeted her at the door; they ran to her as children do, wanting to be cared for; they became her children something alive to come home to.

****

18

*A*mazingly **every child reacts** to a parent's illness in a different manner. Ailey's motivations and daily attempts to help were making breakfast, coming over to see what Jon's needs were, and visiting Lale at the hospital, then continuing these same concerns when Lale was transitioned to Hospice. Poor Ailey—her health wasn't good either. They did not discover to what extent until sometime much later. She did much to conceal the magnitude of her illness—sometimes avoiding the family members for lengthy periods of time, and refusing concerned family visits, even when she herself was hospitalized. She put up a good disguise; she was their dear sister, and they loved her greatly, the family made a conscious effort to understand and honor her wishes. After all what were they to do when she began to refuse to receive their visits?

Jenna and her spouse's involvement, helping with Jon's bath; shopping and whatever they possibly could do, they happily obliged.

Emmy and her spouse Eddie, 'the Chief', as Jon referred to him right from when the couple first married. They dropped everything and drove to Morristown to jump right in and helped with cleaning up the house while Lale was hospitalized.

Even though Eddie's own mother was suffering from Alzheimer's, and his family had to make the decision to place her in a health facility in Charlotte for her own safety, he did not hesitate to split the time he had when he was not at the pharmaceutical company making and measuring Lisinopril, HTCZ, and Hydro codeine medicines.

Eddie has large strong hands and arms; he's tall with a patient disposition, and a willing spirit, so he confessed, "I'm happy and it makes me feel so good to know I'm here and can be of some service in this way for the family—my family." One of Eddie's joys is for someone to listen to him tell his childhood stories. So while he scrubbed, moped, wiped and polished, he began, "Coming up in a house of ten children, my mama made us boys get down on our hands and knees to scrub her hard-wood floors and polish them with Johnson Paste Floor Wax. Then we buffed them until they shined and we could see our faces in the wood. This was done once a month like clockwork. Then once they were so slick we could slide across the floor in our socks, my oldest sister, Vicky would put us out of the house and make us go to play, so the house would still be clean and the floor would be spotless when Mama came home from work. If we wanted a drink of water, she would say, 'You had better use the water hose, 'cause you're not getting in this house before Mama comes home!'"

Emmy found his story comforting; it was twofold—helped to pass the time and besides it provided Eddie an unexpected opportunity to transfer the bottled up emotions he held inside to cover up the helplessness he felt about the future of his own mother's health condition.

****

It was discovered that people can be amazingly good; there were people around, a long procession of visitors the entire time, praying, wanting and wishing Lale well.

Their visits to see Lale at Hospice were around the clock. Aunt Mart, Jon's youngest sister, in her old age said at the end of her visits, *"See you later alligator."* A line that was popular that the two of them shared when they were young girls. Mama's response was *"After while crocodile."*

The men, Jon Cam Jr., Karl and Lewis kept up the areas--duties that are just too strenuous—that women prefer not to have to do, like mowing the lawn, moving heavy objects etc.

While Lale was hospitalized, Jon still needed to have medical treatments at the VA hospital in Durham.

Reynolds drove his cripple father to make the three hours, long odious one hundred, and seventy-three miles trip. Although his physical condition caused his inability to move swiftly, yet his mental ability was strong enough to allow him to "stay on top of his game": Dad informed Reynolds about the correct VA forms that needed to be completed.

As Reynolds headed for Highway 73 East, Jon read, "Once your application is successfully processed, you will be assigned an enrollment Priority Group. Certain Veterans may be eligible for more than one Enrollment Priority Group. In that case, VA will always place you in the highest Priority Group that you are eligible. Under the VA Health Benefits Package, the same services are generally available to all enrolled Veterans. Once enrolled, you will receive a personalized Veterans Handbook, which will detail your VA health benefits and provide important information concerning your access to VA health care."   Reynolds knew that he was doing a Godly act. He said in his mind, "I can use all the "Grace" I can muster, caring for Dad and driving him home."

****

In the meanwhile, Lionel's recuperation was miraculous; it was believed that when that Mac truck hit the side of his car that he and Will road in, he too could have died right then and there, but there was a guardian angel standing in the way by his side, their little sister Sandy Kate, who had saved his life numerous times stood there.

By now, Lionel, through his reciprocal responses while he was hospitalized, he listened to his father, Jon's discourse, and was able to make a valuable enlightened discovery. That particular experience taught him an old saying Emmy heard in a sermon from the good Reverend Dr. Lynch that she shared with Lionel: that 'he could not kick every "dog" that barked at him if he wanted to get to the corner.' It reminded Lionel of the time he took off running after a strange dog standing in his yard that snarled at him. "No you didn't bark at me; on my own property; in my own driveway," he threatened. The seriousness of his chase made all the analytical sense in the world as he blindly pursued, at full speed, the stray animal; he fully dressed in suit and tie. Now retrospectively envisioning the incident, he thought to himself "How ridiculous I must have appeared to my new wife, Leann, as she drove down Brush View Lane entering our driveway to home." It seemed that his recent storm with life taught him to choose his battles more carefully. Unlike the battle at the ball field with Karl when he was shortly out of Viet Nam and still reacting paratrooper like to confrontations even when it came to his own kin. Like war that he so often spoke of changing him, his latest storm—the serious traffic accident that had taken Will's life yet God had spared him, this, he felt had enlightened and, he felt totally transformed him.

He learned and made a good decision that he would choose to hang on to the positive memorizations of his good friend Will and that he wasn't taking any risk of becoming overcome and lost in the aching of his heart and mind about the accident. After all it was an accident—and they do happen. Unfortunately he could not turn the clock's hand counter clockwise, back far enough to change the outcome, because life just isn't that way. So he would have to live with the way it turned out. He whispered, "I am alive, and glad to be this way." He made up his mind to go sit and visit with Will's sister in the coming weeks; offer her some small monetary compensation of condolence for her great loss and pray with her.

****

19

*L*ale's **condition** **certainly** **had** its psychological effect on her husband. Jon's loss of control of his body functions—fecal matter was everywhere!

Poor Rudy had to remain strong in her faith; she was always there to clean up the mess! But her human side had to reveal itself especially when the smell was still so strong in the memory. And the stubbornness was so visible in the memory. Her anger forced to the surface by his hardheadedness—his stubbornness.

"I don't need to wear no diaper." He had said standing there with the strong smell of his defecation oozing out of his pants—dripping down his legs, leaving pools of it at his feet when he walked.

When she told her sister in a telephone conversation, as they talked it was not too difficult for Emmy to imagine just how overwhelming the experience must have been for Rudy. But Rudy was a trooper and did not relent; neither did she hold a grudge against her father; she forgave him in the Biblical way that she professed: "Forgiveness is the gift that keeps us giving, both to Jon and me by liberating my soul from the burden of harboring destructive and corrosive emotions by reflecting a shining ray of God's unconditional love to others through the way I treated him." So she helped him clean himself up—remove the soiled clothes, helped him balance himself into the bathtub to get bathed up; helped him out of the tub and dried down, and then she moved on to the next phase representative of her inner freedom.

Rudy's telephone call to Emmy was simply a need to vent. When finally she realized she at least needed to take some days off—to revitalize her own mind and body, she did what she had to do. Her husband had insisted that she did. It was shortly after driving home from the road in his 'big rig'. He had recently had her car serviced and cleaned and the gasoline tank had been filled, even though it had been late when he arrived home, he had showered, shaved and made dinner of fried pork chops with gravy, green peas from his own garden and steaming hot rice. He had taken over paying all the bills to relieve Rudy who usually did them like clockwork at the beginning of each month.

The daily routine with Lale at Hospice:
Rudy, Topia, and Jenna, were there every single day, and Rudy spent numerous nights, sleeping on a chair at

Lale's side in her room. Topia spent numerous days at Lale's side, and her face wore the pain of knowing what was to come.

Rudy was continuously trying to remain strong, yet the stress was breaking her down too; her husband's concerns—it's too much! He planned to have a talk with his wife, but decided to postpone it until later. And not before calling the siblings to vent for himself his frustrations of the constant care for the two parents— that there needed to be more input from all the members—because there was just so much that needed to be routinely done. He was being the good husband, obviously concerned for his wife's health.

****

The children's morale began wearing down with devastation and fear knowing the inevitability of Lale's serious condition and having to come to terms with the thought of losing her was real. They had been taught that the Father says in the 'Good Book' the anecdote for fear is Trust. Ephesians: No one wants to lose their love ones. Even when it is known that they are going to a better place—in heaven to be with the Father.

****

It soon became apparent that Jon could no longer remain at home alone—as a precaution; the family needed a house sitter, especially one to be there with him when there was no other family member around. God sent the answer to their prayers, a family friend of Rudy, Bernie, repositioned his life to move into the house to reside with Jon so that he could be there in the house at night.

Bernie was reliable and was always there when he needed to be. He did not cause problems or bring strange people into the home. Neither did he seem ungrateful; he had a willing, agreeable and Godlike spirit.

Bernie did not have a steady job per se, to sustain his income; he met downtown with Morristown construction companies that solicited workers to complete odd jobs during the day; returning to the home on time when needed. He became a good reliable family friend. They speculated about the possibility, then decided that he was one trusted enough to possibly continue living in the home once Jon and Lale were laid to rest. And even later when and if Topia moved from her duplex or another family member may perhaps move into the parents' home, Bernie, the trusted friend, would continue living in the home.

****

Lale's condition worsens at Hospice. Many times she did not recognize some of the relatives. This sent real fear through all of them—mental fear that was expressed, that brought from time to time fat tears that watered the eyes and found their way down the cheeks. It was difficult to think perhaps that she would not be with them for long. To put it mildly, it was surreal.

She usually remained in bed most of the day and she slept a lot. Her appetite was good but she mostly had to be fed. Sometimes, she needed a pacifier to suck on because she was a child again and her gums itched. When her pacifier was lost, she often sucked on her fingers.

On one occasion when Rudy came to Lale after work, she found Emmy sitting there at Lale's bedside. Emmy felt lost, not knowing what to do as her mother laid there. But Rudy sprung into action with her energetic self and her second wind. She wiped Lale's face with a warm wet cloth, helped her out of bed and wrapped her arms around her, then walked her onto the porch which extended from her room to get her into the sunlight. By this time Lale was so weak and somewhat despondent. She could not walk and steady herself alone. When the nurse brought dinner, Rudy and Emmy fed her.

On one of her visits Emmy hung a copy of the poem she had written, MAMA YOU, with a photograph of herself, exclusively for her mother. She placed it on the wall at Hospice as a tribute to Lale's hard work and the goodness she revealed over the years to her family.

Lionel and Leann together placed the huge green indoor plants Peace Lilies in Lale's room to give her a continued feeling of beauty and life. The Peace Lily is known as the clean-all, often placed in areas to remove mold spores.

Jon sat daily with worried; sadden eyes by his love, Lale's side, in his wheelchair at Hospice.

He, faithfully and patiently, stationed himself by her side from early morning until it was time for him to force his cripple, weak knees and legs to slowly walk to one of his children's automobiles, to try and lift up his legs, painfully turn his trembling body to manage to sit in the car seat to be driven home again leaving in the late evening. Emmy knew this because she on occasion witnessed it upon delivering him—driving Jon home from Hospice.

He did not desire to miss any time with her. He needed to be there with her, every day, as difficult as it was for him to move around, dress and prepare to get there.

She was usually asleep and the stillness surrounding them was like the whole world was changed now. It was evident that his heart pained—it pained so badly; only he knew how it pained for Lale his love.

****

Preparing to lose Lale did not actually enter into the children's minds or their conversations. Inasmuch as their mother was the subject of most telephone calls, text messages, the visits, and emails; they had hope, they remained optimistic, they knew the power of God's Grace, Hope and Mercy--the hope was that she may come home.

****

Reynolds needed Jon's advice; he desired so much to converse with his father about his life-changing decision prior to relocating for new employment. But time did not permit such an opportunity as Jon was away from home sitting at Lale's side.

Emmy, on the other hand, was totally satisfied with how the University situation concluded. The department Dean sent an email granting her an opportunity to view the content of her personal file which she professed it did not in any facet suggest or name any of the negative wordage alleged in the original email. The PhD of the Department who hired Emmy asked, "What do you desire—what do you want? Do you wish to be called back to the University?"

Emmy responded, "I am a happily retired veteran with plans for my appearance when the curtain opens on the next stage of my life."

They both had a great laugh and made plans to keep in touch and go out to lunch within the next week or so.

****

20

*R*udy's call in the early A.M. was alarming.

"It's Mama, she restless; she's been moaning and groaning this morning."

Emmy responded, "O Lord Rudy. I'll get dressed and will be there shortly."

She dressed quickly, jumped into the Mercedes, and on the way to Morristown, as she drove down 485 she telephoned Eddie at his job to tell him, "Mama is very ill. I'm on my way to Morristown, to Hospice. How soon can you get here?"

Without any hesitation, Eddie responded, "I'll be on my way as soon as I let my supervisor know that I need to leave."

When she pulled into the parking lot at Hospice and parked the car, Emmy stepped quickly out and then into the building. She walked down the hall, practically holding her breath because she did not know what to expect. Before entering Lale's room, she could hear Lale's heavy moaning sounds. And when she entered, she could see her mother tossing in bed from one side to the other.

Jon sat in his wheel chair with tears in his eyes. Emmy hugged him and let out a painful cry, "Oh Lord, O Lord!" She placed her hands tightly over her mouth trying to muffle those screeching sounds with her hands.

Rudy stepped close to Emmy, grabbed her, pulled her closely to her chest and held her hands tightly, "You can do this." She whispered tearfully.

Before she went to her mother's bedside, Emmy could see that Topia stood outside Lale's room with her back turned away from the door. It was supposed that Topia found it so difficult and could not come to terms with what was happening—it appeared the inevitable. Emmy immediately went to their mother's side.

Lale turned over to where Emmy stood. Emmy grasped her mom's left hand and held it and placed her right hand on Lale's forehead. As she stood there at Lale's bedside, and in only a second or two their mother, Lale, in 2010, at age eighty-seven, took a final breath, closed her eyes and she was gone.

Another moment passed and Rudy came to the side of the bed where Emmy stood and asked, "Is she breathing?"

Placing a hand up to her mama's nostrils, Emmy could not feel any breath. Emmy answered Rudy, "No she's not breathing."

Rudy proclaimed, "She went easy." Looking at Emmy, waiting for an accepting response, she repeated, "She went easy."

And Emmy with tears in her eyes agreed "Thanks to God Almighty."

The two of them walked away from Lale's bedside. Rudy left Emmy; she went out of the room and down the hallway to summon a nurse.

She did not go to Jon Cam Sr. as he sat there at Lale's bedside—she was not thinking clearly—Emmy left the room where Jon sat and Lale lay and walked to the outside in a daze—she needed Eddie, knowing he would arrive soon. When Eddie pulled up in his truck, he jumped out and grabbed for his wife and she reached for him.

"She gone Eddie, Mama is gone."

Eddie held onto Emmy tightly comforting her. "I'm so sorry, I'm so sorry was all he could say.

Shortly, the family was being called. Only a few moments passed, then, Ailey came rushing up in her automobile and sprang from the car. "What are you all standing out here like this for?"

"Go inside Ailey. Just go inside." Was all Emmy needed to say to her.

Ailey rushed inside. Moments later, her voice could be heard, "O Lord Mama, Oh Mama! No, No!" Heavy sobs from Ailey were heard floating down the hallway and outside. "No, no!"

As the morning hours moved along, one by one, Lale's children, grandchildren and great-grandchildren began to appear by her bedside with streaming tears and expressions of pain, to see the beloved Lale lying there asleep forever and gone to be with our Lord.

For the most part, they could not say that Jon took Lale's passing relatively well—he was silent. His face lost some of the color it previously had. His eyes seemed helpless, to have questions in them. What will I do now kind of question? To whom will I say good night? Someone he wished a good night who he had known for as long as seventy years.   There was something unexplainable about seeing an old man cry, not the kind of cry that screamed or inadvertently blurted out, it was the kind of cry that was soft and solemn yet intense, it was unexplainable especially from witnessing an old helpless man, their dad, in a wheel chair with tears he wiped with trembling arthritic hands holding a white handkerchief as he sat at Lale's bedside.

As the day fell into night, all the family members, young and old, friends of the family, concerned neighbors gathered in the yard, lingered in automobiles, sat out in chairs, on the porch and inside the house at the home to express and exchange stories of life to "catch up" to connect the dots of each others' lives. They came to sip a taste of spirits; share a piece of bread all in the name of Lale and to comfort one another. They decided and agreed upon one important thing-- bereavement taught them to live and treasure the gift of life.

And later that night to celebrate life and morn Lale's passing in their own special youthful way, the young ones, the grandchildren and their cousins and friends of the cousins dressed in their casual party attire, jeans and comfortable tops, cocktail and vintage black dresses; they went out to the Ozone Club in the Queen

City to hang out, to stay out late as long as they could in the A.M. to laugh, to dance and drink.

Many of the older ones Lionel, Jon Cam Jr., Karl and Lewis, many friends and many of the cousins from the Bent Hill side, fell asleep and spent the rest of the night in Lale's home, slept on the sofa, the floor, in chairs, slept outside in cars or stretched out on top of the covers in her bed fully clothed, just to be close to each other and her. They just could not bring themselves to leave where they felt her spirit lingered. It was too soon to separate themselves from the house and door they had entered and left at least a thousand times or more that held an undisclosed part of themselves, and it was next to where Lale had lived.

In the next two days, Alice flew home from Florida with her husband Allen. Rudy's daughter flew in from Dallas, and son Paul flew in from San Francisco. Emmy's husband remained constantly by her side, and her granddaughter Kate came in from Atlanta with Jon Cam's sons. Raven prepared her shrimp and chicken dish, sent it to the family to share; it represented her concern. She could not bring herself to see Lale's final slumber. Lionel now married his wife Leann and his children and grandchildren stood at his side. Ailey's husband, children and grandchildren, and Lewis' wife and children; Reynold's wife and children, the one from Washington flew in during the evening at Charlotte International and his sons met her at the airport. Jenna's only child, her husband and grandchildren huddled together with cousins, a host of relatives, especially

Jon's relatives from Bent Hill, and friends. Lale's dancing shoes on this side had been laid aside.

****

Visitation and Funeral service for Lale.

Many of Lale's children spoke of precious moments they had shared with her.

Emmy as one of the oldest of the children spoke first; she was introduced by Lionel: her monologue went like this, "Mama was always smiling, humming and creating something beautiful for us and our home, showing her love." She exhibited the lace wedding dress ornamented with pearls sewn to the front. "Lale pedaled that Sears sewing machine inserting her special label in the back neckline, MADE BY MOM. Although the occasion that the dress was make for did not last. The dress with all the ornamentation has lasted. Rest well Mom you deserve it." Then she went to Eddie's awaiting open arms to sit beside him-- rest her head on his strong shoulder to be comforted by the strokes of his hands.

Alice said she was a "daddy's girl." She shared the childhood story of waiting for him to come home from work after she may have been chastised her mom. When Daddy arrived, he said, "Get in the car." Taking her up the street to Mangum's store to purchase something good—ice cream or candy.

Reynolds was hesitant about speaking at first, but with a motion of Emmy's head in his direction, the tug at his heartstring prevailed, and he was persuaded. Inside he secretly knew they all wanted to hear him voice the rendition of his boyhood experiences. All of Jon's son's brilliance was so much like his own.

So Reynolds with a seemingly uncertain yet relieved expression, a chance to express what was on his heart, walked slowly to the center of the floor at his mother's memorial wake and began his reflection and tribute, "As a little boy, I remember…"

Lewis as usual when at a loss for words, mostly chocked up with overbearing emotions, disguised it well by substituting a clever joke.

Jon Cam presented Topia and Rudy with a token plaque representing their untiring love and service.

It is believed that Ailey and Roselyn both spoke making it short and comforting.

It is not certain about Karl and Jenna, whether they spoke. However, Jenna's daughter so eloquently recited an original heart wrenching poem dedicated to her grandmother, reminiscent of her school days when Lale drove the children to school in the family station wagon.

Jon Cam Junior's long-legged wife and three of her siblings from her *famous* entertaining family lifted up a spiritual song "When We All Get to Heaven" in harmonious praise.

Many grandchildren and great-grand children; family members, coworkers, business owners and associates, friends and community members including Mangums the owner of the community store where they bought groceries so many years ago appeared at Morris Town First Baptist Hillside Church to give their condolences, prayers and pay their last respects to Lale and her family.

On a sunny, but chilly September day, at the gravesite of Lale's funeral, everyone was gathered and watched somberly, with visible tear-filled eyes and heavy beating hearts, as the funeral director handed one white dove to Jon Cam Smalls Sr. He held it as it at first fluttered the wings. But it soon settled it wings when Lale's husband gently rubbed its small head. And right before this dove was released to fly up to a clear blue Carolina sky, the funeral director released three other White Doves representing the Father, Son, and the Holy Spirit.

Then the single White Dove, the one Jon Cam Smalls Sr. held, was released representing the spirit of the loved one joining with the Holy Trinity of the three in Heaven. The flight of the doves was symbolic of Lale's release and final journey to the other side.

****

The Lord's Prayer

Our Father who art in heaven, hallowed be thy name.

Thy kingdom come. Thy will be done on earth as it is in

heaven. Give us this day our daily bread, and forgive us

our trespasses, as we forgive those who trespass against

us, and lead us not into temptation, but deliver us from

evil.

For thine is the kingdom, and the power, and the glory,

for ever and ever.

Amen.

Ironically, and most likely it was purposefully done, that Emmy never ventured out to walk the grounds of Hospice during Lale's stay—never looked into other patients rooms to witness their care, or monitor any of the facilities, the nurse's stations, the kitchen, nor the flower shop, none of these areas had the slightest of interest to her while Lale lived.   Emmy felt terribly ashamed. She wondered if her other siblings experienced any similar emotions, but the question was never embarked upon? She admitted to herself, we left our mother in her baby like—dependable and vulnerable state of mind in this place that she herself knew nothing about the day-to-day operation.   How could she. She herself   supposedly   educated,   intelligent   and apprehensive—how could she have been so careless, so removed?   Not exactly a complete 'dust off of the hands' mind –set, but her paradigm had not been peeked to the point of concern in this situation.   Although the conditions would perhaps have remained unchanged, still, these thoughts haunted Emmy—Lale's needy and frail face and limbs, so pure, delicate and dependent, that had once been full of activities strong and outspoken. *This was the heart of the matter for Emmy.*

But with Rudy, Emmy was aware that deep inside her mind, that Rudy deliberately and routinely made it her business to know all of this. She had made it her duty to know, there was *something-* some special element inside of her. Emmy termed it a God-given gift—something only 'HE' could grant to one, something so determined and natural and motherly toward those in need of this kind of nurturing, to seek, to care, absent of condemnation, of pride, of never-ending love.

This kind of care consumed a larger portion of Rudy's evenings and weekends and caused her to place her own needs and desires where she seldom set foot nor spent much time lamenting over that terrain of her life, allowing little time to devote to her own intricate feelings over what she was missing in the meanwhile. Lale's needs superseded almost everything in her life, and she was determined that she would not pass her own family's countless capacity of wants on to her mother. Then there was the constant care for Jon as well. But Lale had had more than her portion of neglect in a lifetime. Yet she still managed to care for *twelve* children. It was a beautiful thing to witness. Rudy must have secretly vowed in a covenant with the Almighty to protect Lale from more of the same concerns in her present state. These forces brought Rudy daily—worn, tired and spiritually focused to Lale's side in spite of what she had consistently endured from her own immediate family—her husband and her employment.

21

*O*nly one hundred and twenty days after Lale went to heaven, and shortly after Jon Cam Sr.'s 90th birthday, he had gone to Mount Olive in the early Sunday morning hours with Rudy. She had arrived at the house smelling sweet with perfume and helped her father bathe and dress. He wore his favorite tweed hat with his suit. Before leaving the house, she had taken her hands, cocked the hat slightly to the side because she told him "It's fashionable Daddy; it makes you look cool." And he had chuckled.

At church it had been a good sermon; although it was a physical struggle for him, even with Rudy's help—he would not have been able without her. He had always treasured participating at the church where his father once stood at the pulpit and preached when Jon was young. He had seen his relatives, the nieces and nephews on his brothers and sisters side, all of this seemed to livened him up—put life back into his weak body, even if only for a brief while the memories lingered in his mind.

Directly after church when Rudy pulled her car into the driveway, Jenna and her husband Jude pulled up behind. They got out and she carried a hot meal for Jon's Sunday dinner. He entered the living room and then sat at the kitchen table where he ate his hot meal. Afterward he moved his tired body to his recliner the usual location that he had shared with Lale, the recliner in front of the TV screen.

Rudy soon announced that she needed to go home to her husband and Jenna went outside to move her automobile to permit Rudy room to back out of the driveway. Shortly afterward Rudy left, Jenna and her husband soon left also.

He could not stay here any longer without her. Later the same evening, while he sat in his recliner the usual location in front of the TV screen, he began calling out to his sister who use to live close by before her demise of some years earlier, "Lizzie, Lizzie, Lizzie," then he began calling her name, "Lale, Lale" and calling Rudy's name, "Rudy, Rudy." It was supposed that he was overwhelmed and disoriented by the events that had gone on during the early evening.

Bernie, the house sitter being there with him at the time when he began calling the names of his love ones, telephoned Rudy and she and Topia rushed into the house to Jon's side, and with a quick call to emergency the County ambulance service soon followed.

Some confusing occurrence having taken place earlier; Jon's wallet with his money seemed to have been missing. At first it appeared that the wallet had been stolen, and he was quite upset about his belongings; he had not managed to settle down from the unpleasant incident. The occurrence escalated when the authorities had been called to the house for fear that a stranger may have managed to get into the house while Jon was away at church—and may have been involved causing Jon panic. Ironically, the wallet was soon located with his money still inside—it had simply been mislaid. Jon's heart palpitated heavily and he was still upset when whisked away to Union Memorial in the ambulance late that night. While at the hospital during the early hours, Rudy later telephoned Emmy in the early AM to inform her that Jon had been hospitalized. And while speaking with Emmy on the telephone, Ruby regrettably in her painful tone notified Emmy that their dad, Jon Cam Sr. had stopped breathing. Only four months had passed since his Lale had left him. So following his 90th birthday, Jon Cam Sr. departed in 2011—his destiny was heaven bound to hold the hands and dance once again with his beloved wife Lale.

****

Emmy remembered when Jon taught Topia the Lord's Prayer in French at the young age four. He didn't know he had taught it to Emmy as well because she was only two years old, and Lale told Jon she was too little. Emmy listened and learned it anyway, although she never disclosed that she knew it to her parents. So at her father, Jon's funeral service, she recited The Lord's Prayer in French for the family for the first time in honor of her father, Jon Cam Smalls Sr.

The Lord's Prayer
(French – "Notre Père")

Notre Père, qui es aux cieux,
Que ton nom soit sanctifié,
Que ton règne vienne,
Que ta volonté soit faite sur la terre comme au ciel.

Donne-nous aujourd'hui notre pain de ce jour.
Pardonne-nous nos offences
Comme nous pardonnons aussi à ceux qui nous ont
eliver   .
Et ne nous soumets pas à la tentation,
mais   eliver-nous du mal,
car c'est à toi qu'appartiennent le règne,
la puissance et la gloire, aux siècles des siècles.
Amen.

Jon Cam Sr. the Army WWII Veteran was saluted and escorted with Pomp and Ceremony through downtown and the streets of Morristown on the way to the gravesite, as the family cars glided closely behind carrying Topia, Rudy and husband Andy; Reynolds and Deloris; Emmy and Eddie, Lionel and his wife Leann. In the funeral limousines behind road Alice and Allen, Jon Cam Jr. and his long legged wife, Karl and Lewis and his wife, Jenna and her husband Jude. Ailey and her husband drove an individual car where Roselyn and Dwayne rode with them and Ailey's youngest daughter. Several cars of grandchildren, cousins and other relatives and friends followed.

In the long black car where Emmy, Topia and Rudy road, this glorified occasion caused their spirits to remain lifted and the love enabled laughter to ring.

It was believed, and it was evident, because of that day, and that moment, via that laughter, in his mind Reynolds came to realize that leaving the family to move far away, even if it meant an economical advancement, he came to realize that it would totally break his as well as everyone else's heart. He could not leave them now. "They need me!" He whispered to himself. Although he oftentimes seemed to isolate himself from them for long periods, he felt that his decision to stay would be all worth it. After all he admitted, he had changed jobs enough for a lifetime, yet now, he had to take in consideration his age—not like before when he was young and could move about from job to job to where ever an opportunity presented itself. He had to consider his wife Deloris, too who sat beside him—she had always had his back—he suddenly realized what he was about to do was not necessarily fair to her, although he knew she would never complain— still it would be unfair to her. His decision felt good in his mind and in his spirit. From the jovial expression he wore, his decision had now already been made.

****

The haunting echo, the saddest sound ever heard, of the official military version of "Taps" played by a lone bugler at dusk, during flag ceremonies, and at military funerals by the United States Armed Forces resounded at Jon's gravesite and throughout the Morristown community of the Hillcrest Cemetery in Morristown.

The Army dignitaries saluted and systematically removed then folded the United States flag that had been draped over Jon's final resting bed. When the decorated female sergeant bent down on one knee in front of Topia, *she* saluted and presented the flag and a customary gold trimmed memorial Military Plaque to her in Jon's honor; once again she stood, saluted and mechanically moved away.

A final prayer was lifted up by the Reverend; the family did not watch Jon Cam Smalls Sr.'s casket lowered as they were aware his soul had previously gone up to the other side and was already there with the mother, his Lale, holding her hand to dance with her among the clouds forever.

****

In the meanwhile, Rudy resumed the Christian responsibility so familiar to the family, and she, along with the help of other family members began caring daily for Topia whose health continued to decline. She had begun to show serious signs of dementia: Difficulty concentrating and planning things; Memory loss and confusion; Short attention span; Lack of motivation and Depression. Doctors diagnosed that her condition was inherited. Topia's condition caused the doctor to diagnose   a period of hospitalization and a series of test. Doctors diagnose the cause of **dementia** by asking questions about the person's medical history and doing a physical exam, a mental status exam, and lab and imaging **tests,** *then she was placed on   a routine of medications to aide her memorization.*

Rudy became her guardian as their dear Tobia was unable to manage her own financial and personal care.

One of Ailey's grown daughters moved in to assist in the daily care of Topia. Bernie the family friend continued to reside in the home.

For Roselyn, her father's words would have been, "Make them prove it! *Fight!"* She knew these were the words Jon Cam Sr. would have given her. Consequently, as it turns out, Roselyn did fight. She hired a top-notch, highly respected and well known Charlotte attorney who had a reputation of going to battle in civil rights issues when it was widely known that some 'big wig' needed a weaker counterpart to be the fall guy or sacrificial lamb for his wrong doings. But she did not have to struggle with her battle alone. She needed her family to rally around her, and without having to convince them, they immediately decide to get involved to support her. They wrote letters addressed to the justice system expounding upon her character, morality and work ethic which assisted in her receiving a 'slap on the wrist' not guilty verdict for missing funds according to the State Commerce Division's Investigation for missing currency, but a guilty verdict of negligence, punishable by a one year probation period was imposed against her.

The investigation was continued for the other company employees who were hired under Roselyn and who were directly involved in the missing funds.

****

22

*R*__*hetoric in the Yard:*__ One year after Jon and
Lale passed away, on this sunny Sunday September
afternoon, to honor the birthday of the late, sweet Lale
and the anniversary of her marriage to her husband, the
late WWII veteran, Jon Cam Smalls Sr., the siblings
decided in jovial telephone conversations, which they
had the night before, to meet after church at the parents'
old homestead where the oldest sibling, Topia, now
lives. Everyone called her by Topia Cee, by her first
and last—complete name.   And most times she was
referred to by the loving CiCi. CiCi was a collector of
objects: ceramic figurines of winged angels cluttered her
counters, Christmas decorations and candy canes filled

her drawers, empty flower pots—small, medium and large lay about in the yard, crystal ware lined her cabinet space, pecans rolled about in the trunk of her car; in one corner of her living room sat a naked mannequin with its arm raised up to touch the sky like Lady Liberty. She continued to be a collector of cats too.

As the family all sat sunning, some sat on the front porch and others in the front yard in the late afternoon, they swatted flies, waived to the neighborhood's passersby; they engaged in casual conversation about nothing of a particular significant value, except they spoke of the parent's gravesite, and the balloons that had been placed there. "Probably put there by Baby Girl; she loves balloons." This revelation made by Rudy in her melodious tone, who sat in a white, plastic yard chair, in the middle of the front yard; she wore a wide-brim green fedora. All of the members were in agreement concerning the balloons with an occasional nod of the heads. "Ruby that hat looks so good on you." "Thanks man." Rudy returns to Emmy.

There was some talk of CiCi's many cats that roamed freely about the yard—Siamese grey, midnight black with blue eyes, yellow stripped. The question was presented, "Just how many cats are you allowed?" Nothing addressed of a confrontational or innuendos' nature, simply a curiosity directed specifically to CiCi. But CiCi sat on the front porch with steady wide-eyes; hands holding onto the arms of her plastic yard chair veering at Emmy. Her unchanging expression seems to reveal her thoughts: the very *audacity* of such a question. With her unswerving stare, which she never found necessary to ever retract even an unspoken threat and her silence, at least in Emmy's mind, she seemed to communicate, "This is *my* house; I'll have as many cats as I please—so back off!" Emmy drops the subject for the moment as the air has become somewhat thick. It causes the positioning of the members to change. Cam lit a cigarette, started to puff and blow smoke into the breeze until Emmy protests, while fanning the air with her hands, "You're **killing** me with that smoke!" Cam doesn't respond, but with his polite grin, showing most of his thirty-two white piano keys, gets up and moves to stand near his SUV, parked at the edge of the yard. He blows his cigarette smoke in another direction into the summer breeze.

Then the subject of the cats soon arose again. Some of the members expressed contempt, (damn cat under my car); some expressed concern (that cat's eye is running)—some express fear and anxiety, jumping from a chair when the cat attempts to rub against the legs. (They get on my nerves-get away from me, Cat!)—Emmy and Rudy agreed the Siamese grey was pretty (is it male or female)? (I don't know).

They talked of cooking, and food preparation derivative of all food groups: from fresh garden vegetables, fried chicken, to seared chicken. Emmy chimed in, "Now that Eddie has his papers in Culinary, there is no more 'simply preparing the chicken,' it's now "Meso Plus," and searing the chicken, rubbing the chicken with herbs, and whisking, and now it's a "Rue," not gravy. I told him, my mama didn't whisk anything. She beat it with a fork in a pot. And I didn't tell Eddie, it was usually that same pot Daddy shaved in the morning before." Laughter was shared, and echoed throughout the neighborhood and up to the sky. The members were in great spirits. Rudy remarked, "You should have told him that Emmy." Emmy answered,

"Some family secrets are sacred." Laughter of the members is heard once more, and the atmosphere is once again one filled with delight.

Rudy, again in her easy-on-the-ear anecdote makes a case, "David won't allow me in the kitchen to cook anything these days. He tells me, now look at that, Rudy, you've messed my food all up. I had to tell him, now, David, you don't know what you're talking about. While you were in the yard, I'll have you to know (she says this time more forcefully) I have marinated and seasoned this chicken and everything!"

Then, somehow the subject of matrimony rose to the forefront. Emmy provocatively makes the asserting statement, "If something, God forbid, should happen to Eddie, I will never have another husband." All the siblings and in-law listened attentively--thoughtfully. Rudy declares, "I'll keep trying; I don't care how many times it takes." Head nodded in affirmation for Rudy's confession of future commitments.

"Not me." Proclaims Emmy, "although I don't intend to be alone, I just don't want to marry anyone. (Murmuring is heard from the group as Emmy continues), I'll have a life-long partner, but…" With these words "life-long partner" her monologue is interrupted with a sudden simultaneous **uproar** from the group.

By now CiCi has also gotten up from her yard chair; she stands silently erect and barefooted in the middle of the front yard, her arms folded loosely across her chest, watching and listening in amazement. She too appears in good spirits, no longer with the heavy artillery face.

Cam asks, "So what you're saying is that you plan to "**SHACK**?!"

Now the sister-in-law, Cam's adorable, long legged wife, who was still sitting on the front porch, jumped from her chair to her feet, and in her usual hoarse voice, as if she is about to witness Emmy's getting struck by lightning yells, **"Oh Lord have mercy!"**

Rudy leaps into the rhetoric again, "No, the man is going to have to marry me! I'm not staying with *NO* man outside of wedlock."

As all the members, Emmy-and Cam's long-legged wife- and Rudy are heard lightheartedly speaking in individual proclamations at the same time in the background, Cam continues. However, by this time, he finds it necessary to preach to the crowd like Papa, our grandfather from the Height. "The Lord God saith, thy shall *NOT* commit to live in a disorderly manner!" Emmy interjects, "The Bible was written by men, inspired by God. God is a spirit." Cam responds, **"Inspired my foot**; God ordered these words written!" Emmy is heard, "You can be married in the heart. The King James version was written so man and woman would marry and then the government could be in their business to collect taxes from them." Cam still sermonizing and interrupting Emmy, **"I- don't- care- what- version- it- is!** "And the government is going to get it *anyway*! The Lord has an order to **EV-ER-Y-THING!**—the stars in the heavens shine at night, the moon comes out at night because of the rise of the tide pulled by GRIVITY!" Rudy is seen, sitting on the edge and leaning to one side of her white plastic yard chair. She is heard in the background, **"Listen to him Emmy!"** Cam lectures, "The gravity causes the earth to stay in place, and rotate on it axis and the sun rises in the east. The trees and the plants on the earth are in order with the seasons: winter, spring, summer and fall. And, *by God*! The Lord ordered the union of man and woman to be married!" Rudy is heard, **"Let him talk Emmy!"**

CiCi finally comes to life. She picks up a plant drainer from the yard and holds it in the palm of one of her hands like a collection plate used to collect money at church. She starts walking around, pausing in front of the group members as if she's waiting for someone to drop a donation in the plate.

By now everyone is in soaring laughter at CiCi's gesture; they are filled with joy of being together engaging in rhetoric like the old times. Then the sound of another automobile is heard pulling into the yard. Their gazes aim when the motor stops, the driver's window lowered, they can see it is one of the grandchildren, Lionel's, who is not present, daughter says, "Yes it's me. And I know you're all saying here she comes— looking and acting just like Lale!" She climbs out of her car to join the group in the yard.

Epilogue

We as a family have not fallen apart. But changing our lives is not an easy task. This emotional change having taken place inside of us is the weightiest experience ever witnessed. We have become stronger because we've had to. The wonder of the Father's love is the awareness that the Lord will carry us through each and every day. We're holding onto each other because God put us here on this earth together, and He put his love in our souls as guiltless children.

Jon and Lale are so present in our hearts and in spirit. They are sorely missed, but their spirits can never die because what God creates is everlasting.

As a family we have managed to remain as geographically close as health conditions and other natural outside forces, like the unpredictable weather, will allow, keeping in mind that none of us are getting any younger and cannot dance at every wedding.

Idealistically, it's felt that life would be more enjoyable if there were more visits to siblings' homes, and more often, but it is just not a possibility." Modern day technology is somewhat of a modern day miracle. The miracle of the "wire" allows us to telephone, email, Text, and visit social media to stay in the "loop" with each other. It's not exactly easy to constantly keep in touch with ten siblings whose roles as mothers, fathers, grandmothers, grandfathers and great-grand's are in constant demands.

Rudy calls Emmy, Reynolds and Alice. Emmy calls Rudy and Reynolds and sometimes she calls Alice. Reynolds calls Rudy, Emmy, Alice, and Jon Cam Jr. Jon Cam Jr. calls Karl and Lewis. Lewis calls Topia and Roselyn. Alice calls Rudy. Karl calls Rudy. Jenna called Ailey before her passing. We
all call 'the Godfather' Lionel. And so it goes.

They Text but Emmy decided "Texting is just too much!"

But during special occasions, most of us do try and make the extra effort to find our way to each other's doorsteps. But when there is a special event, a birthday, an anniversary, a celebration, and when family members are absent, we do not experience fear or paranoia. Individually we are confident in our spirit that we are prayed for in the hearts and minds of each other and we are therefore secure.

We all believe that Jon and Lale cannot help but smile down upon us from heaven because of the way we were brought up under their ideology and Christian love.

Jon and Lale were interesting and complicated parents who came up during extremely difficult times in life. It was difficult to put off short-term pleasures for long-term goals when you practically have no monetary power. But they inadvertently gave us the gift of perseverance in life. They gave us the example of unconditional love and commitment to stay together against all odds through God above.

Thank God for giving the gift of a good memory from early childhood and the comfort associated with these memories.

Following the leave from the University, Emmy remained active as Alumni with the University's Retired Faculty and Professional Staff Association through various opportunities, including the Chancellor's Holiday Party, speaker series, the library events, sports season events and other prestigious campus activities.

Sadly to say, three months following Emmy's decision to leave the University, just as she was about to accustom herself to perhaps sleeping in later than usual, the telephone rang in the early AM. It was a tearful older daughter, Pricilla, calling from Los Angeles to inform her of some heartbreaking news, that her sister, Emmy's beloved youngest daughter, Carmela had passed away unexpectedly while sleeping. As the rule goes, in life, it's almost never a good thing when there is an unexpected telephone call either very early in the AM or very late in the PM. As the day wore on, most of the family, church members and friends, as they received the unfortunate news, extended their support and rallied around her: Topia, Rudy and Andy, Reynolds and Deloris; Roselyn and Dwyte; Lionel and Leann; Jon Cam Jr, Lewis and the wives. Later that same evening, after the call, Emmy and Eddie left the Queen City, literally on the next flight departing for Los Angeles.

In as much as we knew our sister was ill, and she had abruptly brought to an end the acceptance of any family visitations, it was still a devastating blow to all, when the beloved sister Ailey passed away only one year after Emmy's daughter. Yet, we all realize, God knows best.

The need is to present and elaborate on the purpose for Emmy Smalls' approved University Syllabus; which clearly substantiates evidence of her obvious understanding of the genre orientated (type of writing-a category of artistic composition-college types=research, evaluation, reflection, inquiry) multimodal (varied technology use=the value that appears most often in a set of data) =power point, images, charts, graphs, etc) curriculum=subjects comprising a course of study in a school or college and bring attention to what is considered, it would appear, disrespectful treatment of certain groups by the University. Refer to Appendix A.

Appendix A.

Syllabus: Professor E. Samuels' English 1102-999 Writing and Inquiry in Academic Context II.

Spring W/F 11:00-12:15 pm. Friday Rm 576
Office Location: Cameron 482
Office hours: W 12:30-1:30 pm by appt.
Office Phone: 704-978-2345
E-mail address: Esamuels@uncc.edu

Required Text and Materials: *From Inquiry to Academic Writing Text and Readings,* **Stuart Green and April Lidinsky**
Required materials: A three-ring notebook for your Portfolio, and a Spiral Writing Notebook.

You will be expected to make copies of your own writing; and expected to make copies of requested research text to support some Internal Citations.

Course Description: *English 1102, Writing and Inquiry in Academic Context II.* Prerequisite: Passing of English 1101. Students develop an extended inquiry project that integrates materials from varied sources and includes writing in multiple genres. Students write, revise, edit and reflect on the work with support of peers and teacher. In the inquiry-based classroom the instructor as well as the students ask questions and explore answers not preconceived. Students immerse themselves in on-going conversations (Rhetoric) about topics and ideas through reading, questioning, and process writing, which includes initial interpretation— some of which will be recorded in journals that may serve as the foundation for formal essays. Polished writing may assume the forms of presentations, reviews of research, essayistic arguments, or multi-media and web-based projects. Students learn to recognize rhetorical contexts, practice different conventions, and develop a stance in relation to research. Adopting digital technologies to network, compose and or critique and disseminate their work is a part of this course.

Course Requirements: You will work under the constraints of following directions. Students are expected to: Write intensive composition aimed toward developing written and oral communication focusing upon a different genre for A Research Question; An Inquiry Proposal; An Annotated Bibliography of collected secondary researched sources in MLA format; A Position Essay or Research Review Essay; A

Storyboard and Multimodal Project; A Portfolio of semester work including a Reflective Letter is required. Additionally, assigned textbook readings, discussions, Tests, workshops, peer reviews, Initial and revised drafts and Conferences are required. Students will critically analyze, explore and discuss ideas related to our overall theme of cultural experiences, and examine intertextuality of storytelling and the affects of the human condition in our writing, which influence what gets said by whom and how it is said. We attempt to understand connection between primary and secondary sources; and how technology has influenced cultural, social, political and economical relationships as we explore our own writing habits. **Students will work on some assignments simultaneously. Copies of research text to support Internal Citations are required**, and documented correctly according to **MLA** format, typed in Times New Roman **10**-point font, **always doubled-spaced**, and submitted with the initial draft arranged neatly on the assigned due date. There will be some group on-line postings from assigned readings. **Assignments handed in after the class on the date it is due are Late and penalized a letter grade for each class period they are late**. Even when absent, you are expected to turn in the assigned work **on time—so please plan accordingly.** Printing (copying) papers to be handed in must be done outside of class. **Presentations and any other in-class work cannot be made up**. Some in class work will receive only a check for doing them in an adequate manner. All assignments must be completed for passing of the course. **No email** submissions accepted (except for posting requested assigned work). **Use of Computers Policy: Word Processor only. There should be no browsing the**

internet, nor sending emails, and no Texting or Cell phone usage, as this activity is disruptive, and unacceptable.   Major classroom rule: Respect self and others at all times.
Attendance and Class Participation are essential: Students will automatically be dropped a full letter grade at your fourth, and another at your fifth absence. **Six missed classes constitute automatic failure of the course.** If you must be absent, **you are responsible for getting handouts, notes and extra assignments from your fellow classmates.**   Please obtain the **phone numbers** of at least **three** of your fellow classmates on **day one** and arrange a reciprocal agreement to obtain these for and from each other. If a student enrolls after the first official day of class, s/he is responsible for all assignments given prior to enrollment.   **Repeatedly entering the room after I take attendance is unacceptable, as is being unprepared or without having read the assignment. Three late entries count as one class absence.** Much of the work done is **collaboratively**; it is beneficial for you to work with others (your audience) while you are learning effective argument.
Group Work and Peer Reviews cannot be made up. Students who miss Workshop will miss the opportunity for peer and my comments on your work; therefore will need to revise their own initial essay with annotated comments written on the paper and in the outside margins submitted with the final draft.

E. Samuels' English 1102-999 Spring
Revision Policy: Papers submitted without the required criterion of the assignment handout cannot receive a

passing grade. Rough draft allows for revisions, there are no further revisions allowed after the final drafts are submitted.

Make-Up Work

The policy on late work above explains the policies on rough drafts and final essays, projects, daily work, quizzes/in-class work; these assignments are due on their due dates, and no make-up work is allowed.

Extra Credit

I do not offer extra credit.

Distribution of Assignments

Inquiry Proposal (approved) and short Presentation   05% Draft 1 and Revised draft required.
Researched Annotated Bibliography   20% 10% each component.
Position Essay and Reflection   20% Draft 1 and Revised draft required.
Portfolio and final Reflective Letter/presented on Exam day 30%:   (20% Portfolio/10% Reflective letter).
Final Product: Storyboard / Multimodal and Presentation 20%. SB & Multimodal 15% Presentation 05%.
Tests on Assigned Readings   05%   Breakdown of test TBA

Total possible points: 100 Total

Grading policy is based on the University grading scale: A: 90-100; B: 80-89; C: 70-79; D: 60-69; F: 59 and below.

Academic Integrity: See Attachment

Special Conditions: If there is a special need because of a disability, please see me during the first week of class for arrangements. Bring your paperwork from Disability Service

The Writing Center located in_____Cameron 967: I encourage students to visit the Writing Center at various points of the writing process. Carry your written assignment and a hard copy of your essay for which you need assistance. You will need to call for an appointment or stop by in person to do so.

_____**Stude nts referred for Procrastination Counseling may result,** when work deadlines are not met on the dates they are due.

_____

_____

_____

Student Agreement for E. Samuels' English 1102-999 Spring

Tear off and return to E. Samuels on Day one (1) of the class meetings: I (student's name)

Sign_____Print__

_____Student's

ID#_____

Email address_____

I, your name_____ have read,
understand and adhere to the criteria and requirements
for passing **Emmy Samuels' English 1102-999, W/F
Spring**, which is outlined in Samuels' Syllabus for
pages one (1) through seven (7). I understand that late
papers will constitute penalty of letter grades. Six (6)
absences constitute automatic failure of the course. I
understand that I am to produce the appropriate required
copies to support Internal Citations of my researched
text used in my Work Cited. I understand I must
complete all work, i.e. assignments in order to pass the
class. I adhere to the Use of Computer Policy, the
Academic Integrity Policy, Texting and Cell phone
polity, the Printing (copying) papers policy and the
Procrastination Counseling reference.

**E. Samuels' English 1102-023   Spring
Syllabus (Subject to modification)   3 of 7**
Week 1
W 1-9   Introductions: Why study Argument?
/Syllabus-Group interpretation. Sign Contracts.
Icebreaker of Peer partners: Exchange of peer
information. HW: Read: *FITAWTAR* C 1:
"Starting with Inquiry," and-C 2: "From Reading
as a Writer to Writing as a Reader." Be prepared
to discuss key elements of C 1&2 readings.
F 1-11 Discussion of readings C1 -2 and low-stakes test
C 1 and 2. Discussion of our overall theme
and/how we interpret **genres**. Apply: Steps to
Analyzing a Text Rhetorically p38, to **King's
Letters from..." handout.** Distribution of
Assignment: Discussion of Portfolios. HW: Read:

FITAWTAR Ch 3 and 4. Be prepared to discuss key elements of C 3&4 readings. Begin: Write up peer interview for presentation, beginning of class 1-18-13).

Week 2

W 1-16   Discussion of reading C 3 and 4 low stakes test C 3 and 4 – Discussion of our theme as it relates to Writing   Essays. Apply: Identifying Claims to several handouts. Begin thinking about Issues and Questions.   HW: Complete Writing of peer interview.

F 1-18 Discussion of our **genres**: Inquiry Question; Proposal; Annotated Bibliography; Position Paper; Storyboard and Multimodal. Presentations of: Peer Interviews. HW: Read: FITAWTAR Ch 5 and 6. Be prepared to discuss key elements of C 5 & 6.

Week 3

W 1-23   Discussion of readings C 5 and 6, low stakes test C 5 and 6. Workshop/Peers: Create a list of five (5) important Issues and inquiry Question in a Journal entry. HW: Continue to work on Issues and Inquiry. (Include: Present the Issue; Write a clear position; Identify the Reasons and Support; Anticipate opposing positions and objections).

F 1-25 Conference day.*Can meet in Atkins-Learning Database for secondary research Annotated Bibliography.

Week 4

W 1-30   Presentations of JE work/shared experiences/Inquiry and discoveries. HW: Journal Entry work continued.

F 2-1 Review of Ch 3, and 4: Claims in Argument, Issues and Questions.

Inquiry and Discovery/ Problems and Solutions: Proposals and Annotated Bibliography

HW: Generating Ideas / Moving from Questions to a qualifying Thesis/ Finding Sources.

Week 5

W 2-6 Distribution: Inquiry Project/ Preliminary Inquiry Question. Steps. See: Handouts:

Distribution of assignments and guidelines for: Inquiry Proposal; Annotated Bibliography

F 2-8 Library: Next step: Conduct primary/field research-interviews, planed observations, surveys. Explicate the purpose and anticipated audience for the investigation justifying its worthiness for research. HW: Collect and respond to **primary** and **secondary** research—**asking friends and family about your subject.**

Week 6

W 2-13   Workshop – now Revise the Inquiry Question. Why should you continue your investigation? **Distribution of assignments and guidelines for**: Argument Essay. Conduct more Research.   **HW: Write the Proposal-Draft 1, following the guidelines.**

F 2-15 **Distribution of assignments and guidelines for**: Position Essay. Continue Portfolio Entries: HW: Complete the Inquiry Proposal Draft 1 for Peer responses next class. Read: C 7 and 8 Text. Low-stakes test 2-20.

Week 7

W 2-20 Groups - Peer Responses for Inquiry Proposal Draft 1. Portfolio Entries continued. HW: Complete the Final Draft of the Inquiry Proposal for turn in on Friday.

F 2-22 Inquiry Proposal due beginning of class. HW: Begin working on the Position Essay. Read: C 9 and 10 Text.

E. Samuels' English 1102-999   Spring
Page 4 of 7

W 2-27

Week 8 **Unsatisfactory grades due by noon on Web March 1**

F3-1   Discussion of reading: C 9 and 10. Low stakes test. Continue the Position Essay – Due date Wed.3-13:   FITAWTAR pg. 317, "Using and Citing Sources." 319, MLA. HW: Continue work on the Position Essay.

Week 9: **Spring Recess No classes March 4 through March 9.**

Week 10

W 3-13   Position Essay: Draft 1 due today. In class Peer Responses. HW: Revise Position Essay – due in next class.

F 3-15 Position Essay: Draft 2 due today.

Week 11

W 3-20 Position Essay: Final Draft due beginning of class.   Multimodal and Storyboard assignment distribution.

F 3-22 Storyboard and Multimodal product focus. HW: Complete Storyboard

Week 12

W 3-27   Conference Day – Storyboard Peer review.

F 3-29 Spring Weekend no classes   Work on: Multimodal Uploaded in Googleapps. Completed draft for peer workshop review / Analysis Workshop.

Week 13

W 4-3   Multimodal. Should   offer   possible answers / solutions to your questions or may generate even more questions.

F 4-5 Multimodal presentations

Week 14

W 4-10   Multimodal presentations. HW: Work on Portfolios

F 4-12

Week 15

W 4-17   Multimodal presentations. HW: Arrive in class with fully compiled Portfolios for next class.

F 4-19 Portfolio review – Peer response.   Portfolio Letter: Discussion. HW: Write   Portfolio Reflection Letter using guidelines.

Week 16
W 4-24   Portfolios and Reflection Letters due-beginning of class.

F 4-26 Last day of class   *****Workshop – preparing for presentations of Portfolio on Exam day and Rap up.

May 1 Reading Day: No class

> May 6, through May 9. Final Exams – Exam attendance required: Portfolio presentations and Writing prompt response.

May 13 Grades Due on Web by noon

E. Samuels' English 1102-999   Spring
Page 5 of 7
**This syllabus and schedule are subject to modification during the semester.

Twenty (20) Issue questions to consider:

Families, Marriages, and Relationships
   1. What is the status of the traditional American family? How far are we willing to go to find alternatives?
   2. What are the benefits and pitfalls of being married?
   3. Should there be a law to stop teenagers from marrying and starting a family?
Education

4. Can moral development be taught? What is the value of Kohlberg's theory of M.D. for different cultures?
5. What helps students learn and succeed in college? What hinders them?

Crime and Treatment of Criminals

6. How should we treat convicted criminals?
7. What should be done with young offenders?

Race, Culture, Identity and community

8. Ideas now spread like wildfire—mixing and remixing in the blink of an eye; can the idea of intellectual property survive in the age of re-mix?
9. Is the very idea of community an outmoded parochial idea suited only to centuries gone by?
10. Why was the Nobel Peace Prize recipient, Dr. Martin L. King, a Christian minister found unsuitable for a gun permit by Alabama authorities following the bombing of his home in 1956?
11. Lyrics are influencing the culture, but shouldn't the culture be influencing the lyrics?

Freedom

12. Should all citizens have the right to carry a gun for protection?
13. How can we balance security against possible violence in schools?
14. How does profiling threaten civil liberties?
15. How can we balance security against privacy in a technological age?

The Future

16. Reality shows do they reflect real life?
17. What will be the gender of our next United States president?

18. What might be the benefits and downfall of Forensic science?

War and Peace

19. War and Terror-intelligence and security—are we safe?

20. What might help establish peace?

Entering the Conversation of Ideas from the final chapters of our text 12-17: *From Inquiry to Academic Writing Readings.*

12   What it means to be educated, and who decides? 319

13   Media Studies: What can we learn from what entertains us? 419

14   Business: How do we target and train our youngest consumers? 517

15   International Relations: Who are "we" in relation to "others"? 606

16   Biology: How do we try to control our bodies? 697

17   Environmental Studies: What effects do we have on the natural world? 813

E. Samuels' Syllabus: Spring   Page 6 of 7
English 1102-999 The Extended Inquiry Project

Almost all academic writing shares one idea in common: It is motivated by intellectual curiosity regardless of the lens through which it is viewed—socially, politically, economically, culturally—it begins with a question, something we wonder about—something that peeks our curiosity—we consider the question an "Inquiry question." According to our text, academic writing is what scholars do to communicate with other scholars in their field of study, their discipline. Academic writing isn't easy. It uses specialized language and often longer, more intricate sentence structure, which you must learn so you may participate in the different disciplinary conversations that take place in your courses.

The inquiry project invites you to do what scholars do: Pose a question, and join a conversation, listening and learning from others using intertextuality as well as contributing your own ideas.

For this project you will develop a question that looks at a specific idea or issue and how it is viewed or thought of. Your question may relate to our theme: cultural experience, storytelling and the affects of the human condition in our writing, which influences what get said by whom and how it is said. Your question may relate to our readings, writing, and discussions about **** You may develop a question related to your area of study or an interest.

The inquiry project is one extended assignment, which culminates in a researched academic essay of several parts. Each part builds on the one before it. The entire sequence will take the remainder of the semester.

The main steps in the inquiry project include the following:

- Inquiry proposal – proposes a question to study and engages in some preliminary reading. (you will make a presentation)

- Annotated bibliography – Summarizes several secondary sources that address your inquiry question.
- Position essay or Research Review – Presents your research findings to inform, advocate, argue some aspect about your inquiry.
- Storyboard and Multimodal project and presentation – Create a multimodal in Googleapps using text, pictures or images, and audio or video effects to share with your 1102 academic discourse community.

Wherever your interest lies, you will follow some common steps in the process of academic inquiry: First), Develop an inquiry question (your question must get my approval by a due date). You must do some preliminary searching and readings to learn what others have written about your subject; then revise your question. Next), you will gather a variety of secondary research to learn in more depth about the conversation concerning your inquiry. Then), you will write a formal paper to answer your question contributing your findings on your subject. The final step), is your Multimodal project and presentation.

Each step in the extended inquiry will include assignments guidelines, due dates, Works Cited requirements, and Reflections which **must** be followed and submitted on time.

E. Samuels' English 1102-999 Spring
Page 7 of 7

Academic Integrity Statement

The University Code of Student Academic Integrity (Policy Statement #105) governs the responsibility of students to maintain integrity in academic work, defines violations of the standards, describes procedures for handling alleged violations of the standards, and lists applicable penalties. The following conduct is prohibited in that Code:

A. **Cheating**: Intentionally using or attempting to use unauthorized materials, information, notes, study aids or other devices in any academic exercise. This definition includes unauthorized communication of information during an academic exercise.

B. **Fabrication and Falsification**: Intentional and unauthorized alteration or invention of any information or citation in an academic exercise. Falsification is a matter of altering information, while fabrication is a matter of inventing or counterfeiting information for use in any academic exercise.

C. **Multiple Submissions**: The submission of substantial portions of the same academic work (including oral reports) for credit more than once without authorization.

D. **Plagiarism**: Intentionally or knowingly presenting the work of another as one's own (i.e., without proper acknowledgement of the source). The sole exception to the requirement of acknowledging sources is when the ideas, information, etc., are common knowledge.

E. **Abuse of Academic Materials**: Intentionally or knowingly destroying, stealing, or making inaccessible library or other academic resource material.

F. **Complicity in Academic Dishonesty**: Intentionally or knowingly helping or attempting to help another to commit an act of academic dishonesty.

A plagiarism detection feature for courses, built into Moodle, which relies on the widely used anti-plagiarism service, turnitin. Turnitin is a "plagiarism prevention system that makes it easy to identify students who submit unoriginal work. It acts as a powerful deterrent to plagiarism before it starts." Turnitin works by checking your students' papers against a large database of millions of published works, other student works submitted to its database and a copy of the publicly accessible Internet.

****

Following her retirement/departure from the University, Emmy was invited to teach English at the Theological Seminary School of Charlotte by Dr. Kline, the director of the school and member of her church Ebenezer, however, she respectfully declined leaving an open opportunity for future consideration.

****

Emmy was later asked to become a part of the EDI (Educational Department of Instruction) at her church: Ebenezer Baptist Church of Charlotte, North Carolina which was in need or more instructors where she presently teaches Christian Education. Refer to: *Appendix B. and C.*

She wrote and submitted Pedagogy I and Pedagogy II to teach in EDI: *Imagine Your Life Without Fear,* Lucado, Max.[1]

Understanding Christian Ethics, Tilliman, Jr. William, [2]

Appendix B.

Pedagogy: I [1]

Title:: Lucado, Max. *Imagine Your Life Without Fear.* Thomas Nelson, Nashvelle: 2009. ISBN 978-0-8499-2020-2.

Course 105: "Walking Boldly" Instructor: Emmy Samuels. Room 116. Time 7-8: p Wednesdays

Aim Use of the Text: ***Imagine Your Life With Fear,*** **Lucado:** The anecdote to Fear is TRUST based on Scripture.

Objective: To invite and connect every person in America to a Bible-believing church, and ultimately into a personal relationship with Jesus Christ through Imagining Your Life Without Fear: "Walking Boldly." The anecdote to Fear is TRUST. If we trust God more, we can become fear less.

Emmy Samuels. Room 116 / EDI 105 Walking Boldly: Date_____

Our focus: Why Are We Afraid?

Course themes pg. 1-6: You are worth more than many sparrows.[1] God will always be with us.[2] We fear because this sounds too good to be true.[3] But when we fear we disappoint God[4] -when fear becomes worry[5]. We should not fear—we are God's masterpiece. [6]

Fear Knocks: P-7 (Matthews 14:27 NLT) Take courage. I am here. Dee's story: Fear and alcoholism.

Why Are We Afraid? P-13(Matt. 8:26 NCV)

Does God Care? P-20 (Matt. 8:25/ Matt. 4:23/8:16/) Fear not genre pg. 23/24.

The Ultimate Fear P-38 (John 14:1-3 NLT) Pg. 31=Philosophers missed about death.

Fear Not: God's Promise P-38 (Matt. 10:31 NCV) Pg. 38 We are God's masterpiece.

Closed question- remembered data	Open question-discussion and interaction – students generate own questions	Use the space to respond.

Extra space for writing answers

But Jesus spoke to them at once. "Don't be afraid," he said. "Take courage. I am here!" On the passing John the Baptist.

behold, they brought to him a man sick of the palsy,
The Death of John the Baptist. ... c **14:27**

28Then Peter called to him, "Lord, if it's really you, tell me
to come to you, walking on the water."29"Yes, come,"
Jesus said.So Peter went over the side of the boat and
walked on the water toward Jesus.

Matthew 8:26-28New Century Version (NCV)
[26] Jesus answered, "Why are you afraid? You don't have
enough faith." Then Jesus got up and gave a command to the
wind and the waves, and it became completely calm.
[27] The men were amazed and said, "What kind of man is this?
Even the wind and the waves obey him!"

Application: Analysis
Synthesis
Evaluating
*We should focus on some main ideas from "Why Are We Afraid," Pg. 13-19.

- **John 14:1-3 New Living Translation (NLT)** "Don't let your ...
  https://www.bible.com/bible/NLT/John.14.1-3
  John 14:1-3, New Living Translation (NLT) "Don't let your hearts be troubled. Trust in
  God, and trust also in me. ... Read **John 14** Download The Bible App Now.

Matthews 10:31 NCV: Two sparrows cost only a penny, but not even one of them can die
without your Father's knowing it. God **even knows how many hairs are** on your head. So
don't be afraid.
Matthew 10:28-31, New Century Version (NCV) Don't be ...
https://www.bible.com/bible/105/Matthew.10.28-31.ncv **Matthew** 10:28-31, **New Century
Version (NCV)** Don't be afraid of people, who can kill the body but cannot kill the soul.
The only one you should fear is the one who can.
Ephesians 2:10 New Living Translation (NLT) 10 For **we are God's masterpiece**. He has
created us anew in Christ Jesus, so **we** can do the good things he planned for us. God said,
"You are my poem…"

*We should focus on some main ideas from "Why Are We Afraid," Pg. 13-19.

We should focus upon the Thinking Skills such as: Analyzing=(underlying theme),
Synthesizing=

(Can you see a possible solution),   Evaluating=(Determine why people choose)?

Appendix C.

Pedagogy: II [2]
Title: *Understanding Christian Ethics*. Fort
        Worth, TX: Broadman Press. 1988
Instructor: Emmy Samuels: EDI

Aim: Assist in understanding Christian Ethics.
Objective: Teach the thirteen chapter themes from
Understanding Christian Ethics as they relate to the
manifestation and accomplishments of an obedient and
ethical Christian writer.

Reveal the testaments of the Holy Bible (Hebrew 13: V
5-6); Matt 1:18, 20 Luke 1 35)
Prov 8: 22; Wis 7-25-26 as they apply to walking in
God's Words. Divine Ordering of our steps through
Faith and Hope exemplified in intelligence=Wisdom:
According to the *Invitation to the New Testament.*

Course themes (to lead to discussions)
    1. Related to Christian ethical/ positive thinking [1]
      - (A Godly act, and the writing process -
        manifestation of the written work: novels
    GREEN and EMILY'S BLUES). Account of one's
    actions.

    2. God's Promise: [2] I will never leave you
    (Hebew 13: 5-6) Our Conduct is to be governed
    by what the scripture teaches (2 Timothy 3: 16-
    17; Psalms 19:7-14); Psalms 119:1-8, 103-105;
    129-130). Our   Conduct is to be governed.

3. **Walking in Gods Words: [3]** Ordering our steps=Listening to what God lays on our hearts - Listen to his promise

4. **Wisdom:** [4] Jesus is the personification of Wisdom. For the Christian, Gods Words, the Bible is our standard and guide.

5. **The Holy Spirit** [5](Begetter of Jesus Matt 1:18, 20; Luke 1:35)

6. **Response to negativity**/turn into a Godly act. Proper conduct is accepted, rewarded, while improper, unacceptable conduct is punished. (Psalms 1:6; John 5: 28-29; Romans 2:1-16; Galatians 6:7-8).

7. **Divine Ordering:** [6] The use of intelligence=God's leadership=Wisdom. God is accountable to no one because of His perfect character (Job 33:13).

8. **Answering the How Do You Do It? –question. [7] Moral** principles written and unwritten, understood to be the norm in a culture.

9. **Making some sense [8]** in the process, and in the world around us, as we strive to be productive/creating happiness. God's Word, the Bible, is our standard and guide. Our conduct is to be governed in everything by what the Scriptures teach.

(Discussion themes related to the Bible and God's teachings as they relate to our daily lives).

Course Description: Understanding Christian Ethics describes that a set of moral principles written or unwritten, generally are understood to be the norm in a culture. There must be a standard and guide for correct and good ethics, and for the Christian, God's Word, the Bible, is our standard and guide. Our conduct is to be governed in everything by what the Scriptures teach. (2Timothy 3: 16-17; Psalms 119: 1-8, 103-105, 129-130). The Bible is the only infallible (incapable of error, trustworthy) rule of faith and practice.

Course Objectives: Understanding Christian Ethics is s study of beliefs or standards that include correct and good actions. Accountability is being required to account or answer for one's actions and conduct. The biblical concept means that people are answerable to certain human authorities, but, most importantly, to God (Romans 13: 1-2; 14:P12). Proper conduct is accepted, rewarded, while improper, unacceptable conduct is punished. (Psalms 1:6; John 5:28-29; Romans 2: 1-16; Galatians 6: 7-8). God is accountable to no one because of His perfect character (Job 33: 13).

Course Requirement: (Schedule: TBA / EDI Committee – See suggested Text Breakdown below)
Class Procedures: Classes will include readings, lectures and discussion. Attendance will be taken.

> Understanding Christian Ethics provides contemporary ethical issues that are substantive enough for a teaching tool use yet functionally oriented toward the local church.

Text Breakdown: (Thirteen Chapters in the text-can be taught in three to four sessions or more if necessary).

1. Why Study Christian Ethics
2. Understanding the New Testament
3. Living to the Glory of God
4. Ethics of Decisions
5. The Church World
6. Politics and Christian Discipleships
7. Preparing for Disappointment
8. Economic Life
9. Who we are
10. Peace
11. Issues of Life and Death
12. Concerns in Contemporary Life
13. A Christians View

(**Christian Ethics**) According to the Bible, (God's Word, in the Bible) -Jesus Calls Us into God's Redemption Story [1] (God Makes Good on the promises God gave to Abraham and David (Luke 1:32-33, 54-55, 68-73) Clues about Jesus: Faith and Hope of Israel (**The Old and New Testament**) **Too many people are saying I'm forsaken—the Lord says-I will never leave you.** [2] (Hebrew 13: V 5-6) **GREEN reference:**

The story of the creation of **GREEN,** a novel and a Christian writer: Connie Williams (as Emmy Samuels in the narrative) applies **Christian Ethics** to her everyday life.

A New York Agent decided to promote my new book GREEN. They wrote a four page review of it, and said, "Two readers have read the book and we both think it is wonderful. There is nothing that needs to be done—it's perfect."

As it turns out, after some weeks, they (the agency) decided they wanted to add illustrations. (**The World outside of Church**) They learned that I did not want other editors and writers names credited in my book, and besides they wanted me to pay the agency for the changes they were suggesting. First of all GREEN qualifies under a mainstream novel, (over 55 thousand words) adult classification under certain length etc. It's not a children's book.

So I told them, "If changes are needed, I am capable of making any "technical changes" such as elaboration, word choice and weaving." (**Politics and Christian Discipline**) So the BIG NEW YORK AGENCY saw that I was no dummy and they ironically decided: We have decided not to take on any new projects!

I knew God would never forsake me—never leave me. (**Living to God's Glory**) I intelligently transformed negativity into a Godly act. (**Ethics of Decision making**) [3] Divine Ordering from God manifestation=use   of   intelligence=God's leadership=Wisdom.

Wisdom (according to *ITTNT*) [4]: (**Reflection: Who we Are**) is rather abstract idea about the divine ordering of the cosmos and about how we must perceive that order to live intelligently=we walk in accordance with Wisdom. The New Testament writers do not stop with tradition about David and his heir. The Holy Spirit as the begetter of Jesus [5] (Matt 1:18, 20; Luke 1:35). Jesus is God's Son and, as heir of David, epitomizes how God provides leadership for God's people. (**Christian Discipline**) [2] This is the leadership of a servant, a redeemer who gives his life for the deliverance of his people, however. They look to Jewish traditions about "Wisdom" to talk about who Jesus is. Jesus is the personification of Wisdom connecting people to God as they walk in accordance with Wisdom. (Seen as female=she was created at the very beginning of God's creative activity (Prov 8:22) and worked alongside God in the creation of heaven and earth: Wisdom as "a pure emanation (Peace) of the glory of the Almighty…a reflection of eternal light…an image of his goodness" (Wis 7:25-26), who enters human souls and "makes them friends of God" (**Issues of Life and Death**) (Wis 7:27).

Divine Ordering: [6] I indelibly knew that when I walk with God—he promised to never leave me=Jesus' faith and hope. But to know this, I had to order my steps in his words. (**Concerns of a Contemporary World**) Listen to his promise. He had already defeated the devil, so I didn't need to refight a battle that was already won. So I didn't fight with the New York Agent. When, in a phone call, from the agent, I was told "I've decided to not take on any new projects."

I simply responded, "Thank you for your response." I kept it simple, because I know my Lord. (**Christian Ethics**) So I got all prayed up and said. GREEN is about to come out! I went to work, sometimes from sun up to sun down. <u>But He will not put more on us than we can bear.</u> Two months later GREEN went to press under my own publication company AWAP.   She (the book) was published February, 2015 and now available in: Barnes and Noble; Amazon Books; Walmart Supercenter; Book a Million; GoodReads.com; Get Textbooks.com; Charlotte Mecklenburg Public Library and Monroe-Union County Public Library.   He will never leave you=order your steps in his words. Thank you Jesus.

Works Cited

deSilva & Emerson B. Powery. *Invitation to the*
          New Testament. Nashville, TN: Abingdon
Press. 2005.

Lucado, Max. Imagine Your Life Without Fear.
          Thomas Nelson, Nashville: 2009. 978-0- 8499-
2020-2. [1]

Musselman, Reverend W.B. *Bible Expositor and*
          Illuminator. Ohio: A Union Gospel Press.
          2008.

Tilliman, Jr, William M. *Understanding*
          Christian Ethics. Fort Worth, TX:
          Broadman Press. 1988 (Syllabus: partly inspired

by The Woman's Baptists Home   and Foreign
Missionary Convention of North Carolina. "The
Missionary   Training   Instituted."). [2]

The Holy Bible: *The New Testament*. Hebrew 13 V
15-16 (Rev. Dr. Lynch's teaching),
      Ebenezer Baptist Church. Charlotte, NC:
      2014.

Willis, Avery T. Jr. and Kay Moore. *The
      Disciple's Personality*. Nashville, TN:
      LifeWay Press. 2016

Williams, Connie. *Emily's Blues*. Charlotte,   North
Carolina: A Williams Acorn   Publication. 2016.
      ISBN 978-0-692-63019-8

Williams, Connie. *Green*. Charlotte, North
      Carolina: A   Williams Acorn Publication.
      2015. ISBN 978-0-692-322371-7

Acknowledgements

This is a work of fiction, based on a true story, but a number of sources have proved noteworthy, including:

Green, Al. Jun 27, 2009 · **Al Green Love and Happiness: "Sha La La"** Twitter.com/fella262.

"Hands": Williams, Connie. Previously published: *A Sun-Filled Dream*. The National Library of Poetry, Tyler, Chris Editor. Watermark Press,   MD: 1998

Heart Disease Health:http://www.webmd.com/heart-disease/guide/heart-disease-heart-attacks

Honor thy father and thy mother: Ephesians 6:2

Jakes, T.D. *Let It Go / Forgive So You Can Be Forgiven*: Atria Books. New York, NY: 2012.

Shall We Gather at the River? - - CyberHymnal *www.cyberhymnal.org*/htm/s/w/swgatri v.htm

Southern Railway in 1940s. The Georgia, Carolina & Northern Railroad started at Monroe, NC in 1887 and built to Atlanta.

The **Arizona Technical Testing Institute (ATTI)** was established in 1996 for the purpose of raising the professional standards and reliability of materials sampling.

The Lord's Prayer: http://www.lords-prayer-words.com/lord_french_notre_pere.html#ixzz 41BVOAbiE

Williams, Connie. English Syllabi: 2014.

Williams, Connie. Goatology a short story and recipe. © Copyright: 1998.

Williams, Connie. "Lillie" a short story © Copyright: 1998.

Williams, Connie. "Mama Allie's Talking Dogs Fried Croakers in Peanut Oil." First published in *Hungry for Home*, Rogers: Novello Festival Press, NC: 2003.

Williams, Connie. "Mama You. Dedication: All for You Mama." A poem (Audience participation: read at each *) © Copyright:1996.

Emily's Blues
A fictionalized autobiography based on a true story by
Connie Williams

In 1989, Connie Williams gained recognition for her first novel, entitled **Emily's Blues**, a fictionalized autobiography. While a teacher in the Union County School System, Williams founded The Emily's Blues Self-Actualization Project, a program designed to help deter school dropouts. Williams later penned "Emily's Dilemma," a stage play adaptation from her book that was performed at Livingstone College by her students, and received Honorable Mention by the Honorable Terry Sanford for an Arts Education Projects, supported by the Union County Community Arts Council in 1990. Emily's Blues was republished again in 2016. As a writer and educator, Williams wrote Emily's Blues to show young readers how she became "unstoppable" in overcoming an oppressed and impoverished background to get an education and become a professional educator. She received the Arts and Science Council Emerging Artist Award for Emily's Blues.

Emily's Blues is available at stores, online and on Amazon

Kindle

Green, a novel based on a true story by Connie Williams

1996, while a Writing Fellow at Headlands Center for the Arts, Sausalito, California, through an Award from the North Carolina Arts Council and the National Endowment for the Arts, Williams began writing her second novel **Green**, a story set in Monroe, North Carolina during the civil rights upheaval of the late 50s.

      Frye Gaillard, author and winner of the Alabama Library Association Book of the Year Award says, "Good description, good imagery and deliberate repetition. **GREEN** is an intriguing story."

      The late, **Minister John C. Williams, son of Robert F. Williams quotes,** "I believe the work will do great things for young audiences who otherwise would know nothing about the late Robert F. Williams, the Civil Rights Activists. The history is relevant and important today."

Available at stores and online!

About the author

Connie Williams is a local figure known for her distinguished career as a skillful writer of prose and poetry. Until her retirement in 2014 she was an instructor of English Composition and Rhetoric at UNC, at Charlotte; a high school English instructor at Charlotte-Mecklenburg Schools and Union County Schools. Her inspirational, fictionalized autobiography, **Emily's Blues,** tells how a young divorcee and mother of four, went from poverty to a professional and was showcased in the "Dare to Dream Project", Z Smith Reynolds Foundation, 1990. She is the recipient of the Arts and Science Council Emerging Artist Award for her book. Her novel's stage play adaptation, entitled *Emily's Dilemma*, received the Honorable Terry Sanford Award for Creativity Honorable Mention, and was performed at Livingstone College at Salisbury by her students.

Her dedication to arts education and outreach led Williams to create, the Emily's Blues Self-Actualization Project, and she volunteered her services to help deter high school dropouts. The program received the Union County Community Arts Council Grant for eight years at Piedmont High School where her book was used with students. She has volunteered her services to Healthy Mothers and Healthy Babies, the University of South Carolina, at Lancaster; International Young Writers Program, in Charlotte. She has presented readings and facilitated writing workshops at: Barnes and Noble, the Charlotte Public Library, Imagine On, Ebenezer Baptist Church, the Nile Theater, and UNC, Center City Campus at Charlotte; Spirit Square, Charlotte; Afro American Cultural Center, Charlotte. She is a Christa McAuliffe Fellow finalist.

She is a contributing author to the following publications: "Mama Allie's Talking Dogs..." stories and recipes of Carolina cuisine, *Hungry for Home,* Rogers. Novello Festival Press: 2003. A short story excerpt, *Emily's Blues*, and a collection of poetry, *The National Literary Circular:* 1990. Original poetry, *A Sun-filled Dream*: 1989. Classroom consultant: *A History of the World* textbook: Houghton Mifflin: Boston. 1988. Williams is the recipient of the 1996 North Carolina Arts Council Award and The National Endowment for the Arts for a Fellowship at Headlands

Center for the Arts, Sausalito, California, as an eight weeks artist- collaborator. She is a former Writing Fellow of the University of North Carolina, Charlotte, 1992. A native of Monroe, North Carolina, she has eleven siblings. Her parents celebrated their 68th wedding anniversary 2009 and passed shortly afterward in 2010 and 2011 within only four months of each other. In 2015 Emmy started her own publication company AWAP (A Williams' Acorn Publication) and published her first novel GREEN under her imprint; and in 2016 she published a second edition of EMILY'S BLUES.

Williams is a wife, mother, grand and great-grandmother. She graduated from Cal State University, Northridge (B.A. Degree), and the University of North Carolina, at Charlotte (M.Ed. Degree). She resides with her husband in North Carolina.

www.ingramcontent.com/pod-product-compliance
Lightning Source LLC
Chambersburg PA
CBHW051509260626
47162CB00008B/2895